HIS HANDS
could work medical miracles in transforming the human face.

HIS HANDS
could produce marvels of music as they touched the keys of a piano and brought them to life.

HIS HANDS
could lead a woman to the heights of passion with exquisite sensitivity and sensual skill.

HIS HANDS
could—and did—kill . . . not once but many times . . .

Now Ann Kurth tells the story that only she knows—the story of her former husband, Houston plastic surgeon John Hill and the human hell he created. Here for the first time are the full shocking revelations of his life, his loves, his murders, and his sensational death.

But is he really dead—or alive somewhere with a new face and identity?

SIGNET Books of Interest

PRESCRIPTION: MURDER

A TRUE STORY

by
Ann Kurth

A SIGNET BOOK
NEW AMERICAN LIBRARY
TIMES MIRROR

Ⓢ

SIGNET TRADEMARK REG. U.S. PAT. OFF. AND FOREIGN COUNTRIES
REGISTERED TRADEMARK—MARCA REGISTRADA
HECHO EN CHICAGO, U.S.A.

SIGNET, SIGNET CLASSICS, MENTOR, PLUME, MERIDIAN AND NAL
BOOKS are published by The New American Library, Inc.,
1633 Broadway, New York, New York 10019

FIRST SIGNET PRINTING, OCTOBER, 1976

8   9   10   11   12   13   14   15   16

PRINTED IN THE UNITED STATES OF AMERICA

Note

Fictitious names have been used in several instances. They are indicated by an asterisk and a footnote at the first mention. Otherwise, all names are the real names.

INTRODUCTION

by Susan Hansen

For weeks I had planned to get away from the city and find a quiet vacation spot where I could concentrate on a manuscript I was working on. As I pulled into a delightful resort on Lake Travis in Texas, I remembered that this was where an acquaintance had moved, and I made a mental note to look her up for a visit.

It had been ten years since I first met Ann Kurth, on a vacation in Jamaica. In the ensuing years I had heard that she had gone through a terrible situation. She had been married to a well-known plastic surgeon in Houston, and as far as anyone knew, they had been a marvelously happy pair. Then, quite suddenly, there was a stormy divorce, an attempted murder, and finally the doctor was on trial, charged with murdering his first wife in order to marry Ann. I wondered how she had fared through such an ordeal.

After I had settled into my townhouse by the lake, I took a drive around the property, and who should I see right away but Ann, sitting on her front steps. With a big smile and an instant wave of recognition, she called me over; she seemed truly glad to see me. She had changed somewhat since our last meeting. My earlier impression was of a beautiful, intelligent young woman in the throes of adjusting to a life she was ill prepared for. She had just divorced her first husband and, with three sons to raise, was facing the frightening

1

world of a woman alone. Now, as I looked at her, she seemed serene and at ease.

During the next two weeks we spent several lazy days together, talking about the things that had happened in each of our lives since we first met. When we were with her sons, I could tell that she and her boys had a kind of special relationship that comes from genuine pleasure in each other's happiness. Eventually, we got on to the subject of her brief marriage to the doctor. I found her story of this terrifying involvement fascinating, yet so disturbing that I had a hard time imagining how she had survived it. It was like a bad dream filled with many bizarre incidents and traumatic episodes. I could see how difficult it was for her, even after all this time, to discuss the harrowing experiences she had endured.

"It all began in such an extraordinarily happy way," Ann told me. "I knew John had an obsessive desire to possess me, but never in my wildest dreams did I expect events to unfold as they did.

"I had thought he was the most wonderful person in the world. We were so completely happy, up until that night in the car, when he told me he had killed Joan. I couldn't believe my ears. His face was contorted and cruel as he described how he had injected her with a horrible concoction that would mean certain death for her. He really seemed proud and bragged about it.

"Just as I was about to express my revulsion he turned toward me with a wild look in his eyes, swerved the wheel crazily, and rammed the car into a concrete bridge abutment on my side. I was hysterical as I tried to get him to let me out before the car caught on fire, but he held me back and pulled out first one, then another syringe, trying to inject me with a lethal substance that would make it appear as though I had died of shock in the wreck.

"Miraculously I managed to throw him off guard and then at that moment a car came along. If it hadn't, I would surely have been killed. From then on, my life was one long nightmare.

"There are a number of reasons for John's unusual personality. His mother had a dominant influence in the formation of his beliefs. He often quoted her theory that 'there comes a time when some people are no longer meant for this world. Sometimes the Lord sees fit to step in and take them. Other times He expects those of us who know what is best to intercede for Him.'

"John had no qualms whatsoever about carrying out his mother's beliefs. He felt this to be his destiny," Ann continued.

"Naturally, everything I know about John and his life, except for the part when I was there, is based entirely on events and statements as he described them to me. He was obviously aware of the fact that some of his actions would not be sanctioned by the world. Nevertheless, he had an overwhelming compulsion to carry out the beliefs that had been so strongly ingrained in him from early childhood."

After I heard her story, I asked her if I might write a novel, based on her experiences. She thought about it for some time but finally decided she would prefer to tell it herself as it had actually happened. What follows is one of the most terrifying stories I have ever heard, the most extraordinary true-life horror story a person has ever lived to tell.

JOHN

Edcouch, Texas, was one of those crossroad communities that consist of a general store, a post office, some gasoline pumps, and less than two dozen hard-working farmers to support it. The neighborhood children went by school bus to nearby Elsa, Texas, where the grades were combined into two classrooms.

By the year 1940 everyone in Edcouch was feeling some relief from the economic pinch of the depression, but it was still necessary to be as resourceful and self-sufficient as possible. As owners of the community store, Myra and Robert Hill had perhaps the most comfortable, though still meager, existence of anyone in the area. Robert was a mild-mannered man, easily persuaded to follow the lead of his domineering wife. Myra was all business and Bible. She had no time for frivolitics. Every day they awoke before dawn, and as Myra prepared the morning meal in silence, Robert did a few chores around the house and opened up the store.

They had three children: Julia, the eldest, John, and his younger brother Julian. Their childhood was closely centered around the small house and their many chores at the family store. School was an accepted interruption in a life that was otherwise centered around Bible study and work in the store that supported them.

Violin lessons for the boys were among the few luxuries permitted. Their squeaking attempts at practice caused amused laughter among the contemporaries who often hung around the store for entertainment. In that part of Texas the days were long and hot, and the nights passed with scarcely a breeze to fan the thoughts and dreams of these people, whose austere lives seemed empty of hope or desire. Nonetheless, Myra Hill had a strong desire for better things, but no means of getting them except through her children. "Get your lessons, boys, and one day you can go to the university and gain the means to a finer station in life. Practice your music, and doors will open that will lead you to the better things in this world." So the boys were groomed for a better day, while poor Julia was destined to prepare the meals and do the laundry.

During their childhood, there were no idle moments, no laughter, no show of affection to detract from the pursuit of the ideal their mother held out to them. At first, the children had been an annoyance to Myra, and when they were small and under foot, she found the best way that she could cope with their presence was to lock them all together in their bedroom behind the store. This was the only life they knew. Their parents were busy every moment in the store. On the rare occasions when the family went out, a harness with a leash seemed to Myra the best way to control the two energetic boys, while Julia trailed dutifully beside her mother.

Every Sunday Myra got out their best clothes and insisted that each child dress quickly for Sunday school. She taught a class of young people and was relieved to be free of her own when they were left at their class. Robert used this time to keep his accounts and secretly enjoy a cigar on the back porch before his wife and children returned from their Sunday ritual.

The world of music was the sole escape open to the boys. The only time that was theirs to enjoy was when they were allowed to practice. They studied first the violin, then the piano, and they found their greatest satisfaction in joining forces to play piano duets. The children at school were given to giggling at the two brothers, who were inseparable, and whom they considered effeminate.

One day when his parents were occupied with inventory, John found himself alone with a friend of Julia's, who had come to the store on an errand. She asked him if he wanted to kiss her. John was embarrassed and scarcely understood what she meant. The next thing he knew, she had taken down her underwear and was reaching into his clothes. Confused and passive, John watched as she continued to pursue her interest in his body. At a crucial moment, his sister opened the door, took one look, and ran screaming to their mother. The episode brought a harsh reprimand from Myra, who was a strict disciplinarian. She forced John to remove his belt, and she proceeded to blister his bottom unmercifully.

Julia scolded her brother for his naughtiness, and that night Julian was full of questions. He crept into John's bed, and while the house was quiet and the family asleep, the two boys spent long hours exploring the possibilities of the game to which the little girl had introduced John. But one thing was certain: John knew he had done wrong to touch a girl or let a girl touch him. His mother's furious reaction had left an indelible impression.

Meanwhile, spurred on by their mother's relentless drive, the Hill boys became accomplished musicians. Their school marks were exceptional, and when both chose to go to their church college in north Texas to prepare for medical careers, Myra knew it marked the beginning of their ascent to a "higher station" in life.

After John had completed his basic courses he decided he wanted to go on to study plastic surgery. Julian was fascinated with psychiatry. Both boys won scholarships to Baylor Medical School where they planned to pursue their special interests. Julia remained at home busily tending the store with her parents.

After the brothers were accepted for advanced studies, they moved to Houston where they shared a dormitory room close to the medical school. The work was hard, and the Hill boys seldom had any spare time. When they did, more often than not they went to visit Professor Arthur Herzfield, who had taken an interest in them. At his home they spent hours playing the piano and listening to records.

One evening the professor invited the boys to be his guests at a concert in Houston at which the great pianist Artur Rubinstein was to play. It was a highlight in their lives; the evening was stimulating, the music inspiring. John and Julian hoped they would be invited back to the professor's home, as they were eager to imitate the piano technique they had so admired that evening.

Instead, however, after the concert some friends invited the professor to a party at their home, and he insisted that the boys accompany him. They found themselves in an unfamiliar part of Houston called River Oaks. As they drove down the boulevard, they noticed huge mansions with beautifully manicured lawns. This was a world totally foreign to the Hill boys, and they were awed by the magnificence of their surroundings. The party was in a house of immense proportions that stood at one end of the street. As they shyly tagged along behind the professor, John and Julian entered a world they had never dreamed of seeing.

Inside, a group of people were discussing the Rubinstein concert. The professor commented on his young friends' talent and insisted they play for the guests. John sat down at the piano with confidence, beginning to play the last Rachmaninoff selection they had heard that evening. The party of music lovers was astonished at the ability of the studious young man, whose style was not unlike that of the maestro they had just heard. Soon Julian joined him, and together they played one of their duets. The group gathered about, enjoying the music and requesting selections. At one point, Julian shyly left John to play solo some of the numbers Julian was not familiar with.

While he was playing, a striking blonde girl joined John on the piano bench. "Could you play the 'Moonlight Sonata'?" Without saying a word, John finished the étude he was playing and launched into the sonata she had requested. He became more and more self-conscious as the girl sat there watching him. When he finished, she gave him a dazzling smile and said, "You're marvelous! Come, have a glass of champagne with me."

As they were being served, John studied this girl who had rescued him from the spotlight. She tossed her blonde hair, tied back in a ponytail, and said, "I'm Joan Robinson. What's your name and where have you been hiding?"

John introduced himself and explained that he didn't actually know the host and hostess, that he and his brother had come to the party with their friend, the professor. "Well," Joan giggled, "you don't have to know them now you know me!" and she took John by the hand and led him out through the glass doors onto the terrace. John felt giddy and lighthearted as the two of them ran along the lawn holding hands.

Joan stopped at the adjoining residence and said breathlessly, "This is my house, and I want you to come to a party here next Saturday. Promise?"

"Well, I don't think I can because I have no way to get here. I live at the dorm at Baylor and go to medical school. Besides, I usually have hospital duty Saturday night."

"Not this Saturday! I'm having a party for my birthday and you *have* to come. I'll pick you up myself." The party next door was breaking up, and John said good night to Joan, after arranging where they would meet the next Saturday.

It had been an unforgettable evening! John stayed awake for an hour thinking about the concert and the beautiful girl he had met. And to think he would be seeing her again for her party!

He was waiting nervously the next weekend when Joan drove up in her convertible. She laughed and chatted happily all the way to her house, putting him at ease. Although it was not quite so overwhelming as the house where they had met, Joan's home was certainly more spacious and comfortable than any John had ever known, and he felt completely out of place. Joan enthusiastically introduced him to her parents and friends. Then she led him to the game room where there were hundreds of trophies in glass cases. Over the mantel was a striking photograph of Joan astride a horse. She laughed at his expression of amazement. "Oh, that's my horse, Beloved Belinda; my father just gave me another one for my birthday. We'll go to the farm tomorrow and I'll show you."

The next day Joan came by and took John to her horse farm. He pretended interest as she showed him her horses; noticing his self-consciousness, Joan rushed to put him at ease. "Let's go for a drive," she said, and slid over so John could take the wheel. John had never owned a car, and had driven his father's old Chevy only on rare occasions. He found as he took the wheel of the car that it gave him a strange sense of power.

A whole new world was opening for the earnest medical student. Soon he was as busy with Joan and her social whirl as he was with his studies. Since his parents had written that they were unable to send the money he needed to continue studies in his specialty, John sought Professor Herzfield's advice about financial aid. The conversation turned to Joan, and the professor mentioned that she was a well-known equestrienne and that her father doted on her. "You ought to marry a rich girl like that," he observed. "Then you wouldn't have to worry about finding another scholarship."

The party routine with Joan was beginning to interfere with John's studies. One evening when she came by for him, she found him sullen and quiet. As she slid over to give him the driver's seat, he said: "Let's don't go to the movies, Joan, I really need to get back early and study tonight."

"Oh, John, don't be a wet blanket. I want to have fun and you're so serious."

"I'm sorry, Joan, but I've *got* to study tonight. I have an interview tomorrow for a grant that may help me through the rest of my internship and residency. It will mean I have to give most of my weekends to lab work, but I hope they'll accept me in their program. I want to go into plastic surgery, and this is the only way I can figure to do it. If I can't get the grant, I'll have to finish and go into general practice."

"Oh, John, don't do that! And don't tie yourself up with all that time in the lab on weekends. We could get married; then Daddy could help you through the rest of school so you can go on to plastic surgery the way you want to. We could live upstairs at my house; I'll get up early every morning and take you to class." She leaned close and put her head on his shoulder.

John couldn't believe what she was saying. He had never imagined a solution like this, but as he ran through the possibilities in his mind, he realized Joan was serious. He pulled over and stopped. "Joan, you don't mean that. You don't know what it would be like to be married to a med student. I hardly ever have any time for fun. Besides, I never have any money to do all the things you like. I had to borrow from Julian just to take you out tonight."

"Oh, John, that's no problem. We could be together every night, and I'm busy riding and at the farm all day anyway. Let's do it!"

"Joan, we scarcely know each other. And I have at least four years of study ahead of me. And then setting up a practice will take all my time."

"Oh, don't be silly," she laughed. "We'll be able to go to the symphony and parties and horse shows whenever you want. Mother and Daddy think you're just great.

Let's go tell them now." She gave him a big kiss and ran her hand through his hair.

It was all happening too fast, John thought. What was he going to do? "But I don't think—"

"Don't argue, John, I've already decided," she interrupted. "Let's go tell my folks."

In a daze, John started the car and drove to her house. Joan took his hand as they burst into the den. "Mother, Daddy, John and I are getting married!"

"Well, well, honey, I declare," Mrs. Robinson beamed delightedly.

"Now, see here, young man, I intend to see you take mighty good care of my daughter, understand?" Despite his words, Mr. Robinson was all smiles. "When is the happy day? We'll have to make it soon, Joan, before your horse show in North Carolina next month. Now, let's see, have you two little lovebirds thought about where to live?"

"Uh, well . . ." John stammered.

"Daddy, could we have the upstairs here? John doesn't have much money and he has to get through the rest of his internship; then he wants to specialize in plastic surgery!"

"A *surgeon,*" Mrs. Robinson mumbled. "My little Joan married to a handsome surgeon. Oh, Ash, isn't it just too good to be true?"

"Yes, yes, of course. Now, boy, don't worry about money or anything. Of course you can live here. That way Joan won't be alone when you're at school or at the hospital. You know, I started pre-med myself, years ago, before I stumbled into the oil business in Louisiana. Then I met Rhea here, and we decided to get married. But you won't have a worry in the world. The good Lord has taken mighty fine care of us, and while I'm not as rich as some of our neighbors, you and Joan can certainly be sure of no money problems. That's just fine. Just fine. Well, when is the big day? I'm sure your people will want to come over here and meet your new family. Where did you say they live?"

"Edcouch, sir. It's about twenty miles from Harlingen, Texas."

"Oh, sure, I used to have a friend that did some drilling near there. Your dad in the oil business, son?"

"No, my mother and father just have a small country store."

"That's fine, boy. Just fine. There's no finer folks in the world than just good old country people. Now you phone 'em and ask them to come up here. Why, we'll have a round of parties that'll knock their eyes out."

"Well, uh, Joan, do you think we should plan to wait till summer, maybe, and . . ."

"Oh, no, John, I have horse shows all spring and summer; I'll be too busy for all the parties before the wedding. Let's just have a garden wedding, and Mom and I can plan everything before I have to leave for North Carolina. Can we, Mama?"

"Surely, darling. Let's have a garden ceremony. My roses will be so pretty in about three weeks."

"Just think, John, a garden wedding in the spring." Joan perched on the arm of his chair and rumpled his hair. "Let's fix some coffee, Mama, and leave the men to talk over their business."

Alone with Mr. Robinson, John had a minute to visualize how his parents would react to all of this. Pleased, certainly. Surely they would be glad to have him marry such a charming girl. Wouldn't they be glad of no more money worries? And Julian—wouldn't he be surprised! It had all happened so fast.

Mr. Robinson was talking about horse shows; John nodded politely, then admitted, "I'm afraid I don't know much about horses, sir."

"No need to, boy. I guess Joan and I have about the finest show horses in this part of the country. I wouldn't be surprised if she takes a first in Madison Square Garden this year. You can't learn about horses from a better teacher than Joan. I've seen to that. She's had nothing but the best money could buy since she was three years old and I set her astride her first pony. Oh, well, that's of no interest to you, boy. Now tell me, what are your plans?"

"Well, as Joan said, I intend to go into plastic surgery."

"A surgeon. Good Lord, boy, I'm proud of you. Why, that's just marvelous. Now that's what I like, a young man who knows what he wants to do and doesn't let anything stop him. You'll go to the top, boy. I'm sure of that. Why with all our connections, you'll have the finest practice of any doctor in Houston."

Joan and her mother returned bringing coffee. "John, let's call your folks now. Mother and I have decided on the week after next. The garden will be perfect and we'll have a week to honeymoon before I leave for my horse show."

"But I have finals in five weeks. Anyway I'm not sure I can get off."

"Oh, John, you don't have to worry about finals. I'll be gone to North Carolina—you can study all that last week. Isn't it perfect! I'm so excited! Here, call and tell your folks they've got a wedding in the family." She laughed and handed John the telephone.

His parents could hardly believe the news. John hurried to get off the phone, but not before Joan had taken the receiver out of his hand. "Hi there, Mr. and Mrs. Hill. This is Joan. Aren't you excited? I just can't believe it. We'll tell you when all the parties are as soon as they're planned. I can't wait to meet you."

Two days later John had a letter from his mother.

Dear John,

We don't know what to make of that phone call. Please write us a letter and explain how you plan to support a wife and yourself, and go through the rest of school. Pop and I have worked too hard to put you where you are to see it thrown away. And who is this Joan? We never even heard of her. Sit down and write a letter to explain yourself. I will be waiting for your reply. On no account will Pop and I come to Houston for any party or wedding. We are working people. John, I want you to reconsider this. The Lord didn't intend that you should reap your harvest until you plow a little.

Now just back off. Pop and I are sorely disturbed. We expect you to finish just as you started. Then it will be plenty soon to start making any plans to marry. Remember there's Ida Lou Macy. Folks here always thought you two would make a fine pair. Her mother is in my Women's Christian Bible Study class and not a meeting is held but that she says, "Tell me about John and Julian."

We expect better things of you, John, Pop and I do.

We are waiting for your letter.

Your devoted,
Mother

By the time John received his mother's message, the Robinsons had already announced Joan's engagement. The announcement, with her picture, had appeared in the papers, and the round of teas and bridal showers had begun. After cutting out Joan's picture from the Sunday papers, John sat down and wrote his parents a letter.

Mom and Pop,

You will see by the newspaper clippings that Joan is a beautiful girl and an accomplished horse-woman. I have always held the desire to marry a girl who could accommodate herself to being the wife of a doctor and still be a person of note in her own right. Joan is continually busy with her show horses and is already well known and established in her own field. We are in love and plan to be married on the 10th of this month.

Her father and mother said you could stay at their house. Joan and I will live there after we return from our honeymoon.

The grant I told you about has all been arranged, so don't worry about that.

I know this is a sudden thing to spring on you. Julian will vouch for the fact that Joan is a charming girl that you will be proud to claim as your daughter-in-law.

The wedding invitations are in the mail and Joan is sending extras to you to give any of your friends there.

There is a party at the Robinsons the night before the wedding. Just go to Julian's dormitory, and he will take you to their house.

> Your devoted son,
> John

John was learning to feel more comfortable with Joan's circle of friends. There was no trick to it really; all they ever talked about was horses and parties. The days flew by, and somehow Joan and John were never alone. He thought they ought to have a serious talk, but he just never seemed to find the opportunity. The round of parties was endless, and Joan was like a little girl opening all the wedding presents. John hoped fervently that his parents wouldn't let him down, although he knew they couldn't really be expected to understand. After all, he had a hard time believing it all himself. Julian had been wide-eyed: "Good heavens, John, those are real rich folks. You'll get so snooty I won't know you."

John blushed. "I really hadn't expected any of this, but Joan is a strong-willed girl. By the way, Julian, you'll have a chance to meet lots of her friends at the party the night before the wedding."

The Hills reluctantly packed their best Sunday clothes in the Chevy and set out for the wedding in Houston. "It's against my best judgment, Robert. Come along now, Julia."

"Oh, Myra. The boy is of age. Let him be the one to decide."

"The boy isn't a man yet. And he's taking on the responsibilities of a man."

As they were backing out of the driveway, they noticed the postman. "Got mail for you, Rob," he said, and handed Mr. Hill a letter.

Hill gave the letter to his wife. "You see about it, Myra." She opened the envelope and took out a folded sheet:

> Dear Mr. and Mrs. Hill,
> You don't know me, but I understand you are fine Christian folks. As I hear it, your son is about to marry Joan Robinson. Before he commits himself, I suggest you become acquainted with the facts.

As Mrs. Hill unfolded the letter, a picture fell out: a man in a striped prison uniform with numbers underneath. At the bottom, penciled crudely, was the name Ash Robinson.

"Lord have mercy, Robert. This means the man is a crook or a convict. He's the father of this Joan person John is supposed to marry. We *must* stop our boy." Her tightly pressed lips and grim expression left little doubt that she was determined.

When they arrived at Julian's dormitory, Mr. Hill never said a word. But Myra showed Julian the letter and the picture, and told him: "Julian, we must prevent this marriage."

"Well, Mom, I guess it's just about too late. They're real rich people and they seem nice enough to me. How do you know who sent that? Could be it's just a crank letter."

Myra was stony-faced. She grabbed Julia by the hand. "Don't you have anything to do with these people, you hear?" By the time they reached the Robinsons' house, Myra was fuming. "I knew it; this girl has just tricked him. We'll see about *her*."

The door opened, and there were John and Joan, all smiles, in a crowd of people. Mr. and Mrs. Hill barely spoke as John introduced Joan and the Robinsons to his family.

"John," his mother said firmly, "I need to talk to you."

"Certainly, Mom, we'll have a good visit tomorrow before the wedding." He was beaming, trying to cover his embarrassment at his mother's unfriendly manner.

Her voice lowered and she grabbed his arm. "I mean *now*, son. The Lord works in strange and wondrous ways. And He has seen fit to send a message to Dad and me. We won't let you go through with this, John." Her stern deep voice carried through the hall. He was humiliated! Mr. and Mrs. Robinson were trying to get them out of the entry hall and into the garden where all the guests were assembled. But Myra wouldn't turn loose of John's arm. "I want a word with you, in private, son." Mr. Hill was standing by, tight-lipped. He didn't like these scenes. Myra was always the spokesman for the family and he was going to let her handle this situation too.

Joan smiled, "Mrs. Hill, why don't you come to my room and freshen up. Come on, John, you all can have a little visit. Oh, Mrs. Hill, I'm just so glad you're here. I'm so excited. Just think, John and I will be married this time tomorrow."

Steely eyes turned to Joan as the bedroom door closed. "Now just a minute, young lady. I'm just a bit excited myself, and it's not from being happy over any wedding, either." She turned her back on Joan and faced her son, who was helpless to understand, much less explain, his mother's rudeness.

"John, this came in the mail. And just in time, I'd say." She handed John the letter and the picture. Joan saw the picture and exclaimed: "Why, that's Daddy! Let me see that letter, please!" Tears filled her eyes. "Mrs. Hill, I'm just so upset I don't know what to do. There are just an awful lot of mean people in this world. I've seen that picture before. Once when I won a trophy in a horse show, the people whose daughter lost to me passed this same picture all through the crowd. They were jealous spiteful people who made up a lot of mean, hateful things to say, just because I won and they were bad losers." She ran from the room and came back with her father. "Daddy, tell Mrs. Hill this is a bunch of lies," she cried.

Ash Robinson closed the door and put his arm around Joan. "Baby, what's all the upset. Why, you've got a party going on downstairs." He glanced at the stern Mrs. Hill as she handed him the letter and picture in silence.

"Oh, good heavens. Why, this is ridiculous! John, you know what we're like. Mrs. Hill, there are some people who unfortunately kept their daughter competing against Joan for years, and the poor child was a born loser. Finally, in desperation, I guess, they started spreading all kinds of bad stories about me, trying to discredit us, I guess, in the eyes of the judges." He waved expansively. "You don't think for a minute we could have acquired this position in life and the respect we enjoy in Houston society if that kind of thing held one word of truth, now do you? Well, my goodness, you should have come right to me with that, and I could have saved this needless grief."

He put an arm around Mrs. Hill, who stood stiffly, unblinking. "Come on to the party now, 'Myra,' is it?

You've got two mighty fine sons. And I want to meet your lovely daughter. Then I want to show you around. You and Mr. Hill are to make this your headquarters. Why, we're just so proud of these young people, and so pleased your John will be our son. You know, he'll have it made. Why, with all the friends we have and the place we enjoy in the horse show circles here in Houston, John will have a practice that will be the envy of all his friends. And Julian, we'll watch out for Julian. Charming boy. Joan, now you all get a smile on. Come along, John, Myra, the photographers are waiting, and Rhea's got a spread down there that will knock your eyes out. I bet you don't throw parties like this down there in the valley, now do you, Myra?" And he led Mrs. Hill back to the festivities—not happy, not really convinced, but at least going through the motions.

The Hills were swept up in the confusion of all the guests. Several people tried, unsuccessfully, to become acquainted, but found them rather quiet and uncommunicative, to say the least. In the end, the wedding was dutifully attended, and the happy bride and groom left for a honeymoon in Galveston, driving off in Joan's convertible.

"Where'd he get that?" Myra nudged Julian.

"It's Joan's car, Mom. Come on, let's go get some cake."

"No, no. I think Dad and I will just take our leave now. We were here just for John. But he's gone off now, Lord help him."

It was when they were alone for three days by the Gulf of Mexico that John realized he was with a bride he scarcely knew. They had seldom spent any time together without being surrounded by friends, usually at parties. Joan kept up a constant chatter about the upcoming horse show, her beautiful wedding and the garden reception afterwards. On Sunday she had room service bring the Houston papers and she pored over the pictures and writeups of their wedding.

When Joan suggested they go back Sunday afternoon, John was really glad. He had all but abandoned his studies, and he knew he had to really cram for his exams when they returned. He couldn't get started too soon, and he still hadn't moved his books and clothes to the Robinsons' house.

In the months that followed, the routine became establshed and more comfortable for John. Ash Robinson had given the couple a bank account with five thousand dollars, so, as promised, John would have no financial worries. Joan spent her days at the farm, riding and grooming her horses. She lived for the horse shows and was away competing every weekend during the spring and summer. Her father and mother were more than kind to their new son-in-law, and John grew to appreciate the fact that he now had time to pursue his medical studies without the worries of looking for a grant or another scholarship.

Their friends were an odd assortment of Joan's rather masculine girl friends who seemed more interested in horses than people. Julian and Professor Herzfield came over occasionally, and the brothers enjoyed their time together at the piano in the game room. And season tickets to the symphony added to John's happiness. All in all, it was pleasant for John—an easy, carefree, and comfortable kind of existence that he had never had. Certainly his plans to practice plastic surgery seemed less remote than they once had.

John spent three afternoons a week in the office of one of the most prominent men in his field. Mornings included studies and rounds with the leading surgeons, as well as actual operating room experience, which he found fascinating. He could hardly believe the ease with which he accomplished procedures that had only recently been perfected. As his confidence and poise increased, he began to enjoy a feeling of well-being he had never before known. He seldom heard from his parents, and they never again came to visit. Yet he was sure that in time they would become more accepting and proud of their son's success.

Ash told his son-in-law he thought he should be in practice alone. "Get yourself a really nice office, John. Don't stay in there working for that doctor. A man needs to make his own way. Why don't you look over in Herman Professional, and pick out some space for a nice suite of offices there?"

When after several years the Robinsons found they were to be grandparents, they were both elated. John was pleased, and he thought a child might bring his parents into the closer relationship he had hoped they would have with Joan's family. Joan, however, was uncomfortable and unhappy at not being able to ride her horses. She endured the pregnancy with an air of petulance, hoping the baby would come early so she could at least attend the Post Oak Show in Houston. It was the event she most looked forward to, and sitting on the sidelines had been a less than happy experience for her.

Finally, when little Robert Ashton Hill was born, everyone was relieved and happy. Joan had a slight infection and couldn't leave the hospital as soon as she planned, but John visited her often and tried to keep her cheerful. The last night of the Post Oak Show, Joan's father came in and told her about the final events. When she heard that her closest rival for years had walked off with three first places, she burst into tears. She grew antagonistic when the nurse brought the baby around to be fed. "You do it, I'm too tired," she said, and turned her back to hide the tears. She held out for the next two feedings, and finally her doctor talked it over with John. They decided that even though she probably should remain in the hospital a few days longer, her morale was so bad that it would be best to let her go home early.

As soon as Joan was able to go back to the farm, there was a marked change. Although she couldn't ride for six weeks, she could watch while the horses were being exercised. She and her father spent hours at the farm every day, planning for the horse shows she would soon be entering.

A nurse was hired for the baby, and Mrs. Robinson was delighted to oversee her grandson's care. Meanwhile John was busy with his new practice. There was a shortage of plastic surgeons in Houston, and his popularity was assured.

One evening, when little Robert was nearing school age, Ash mentioned to his daughter that the house down on the corner of the next block was for sale. "Joan, I want you and John to go down there and look at it. After all, you all need a place of your own to raise Robert." The real estate agent was delighted to show Dr. Hill and his wife the beautiful house; Mr. Robinson had already called her about it, and said he surely hoped the children would move close by.

It was even more attractive and pretentious than the Robinsons' house, more like the other colonial mansions that graced either side of the boulevard. Certainly it was in the best neighborhood, and little Robert could go to River Oaks School, just a couple of blocks away. Joan was delighted at the prospect of a place of their own, and she assured John that her father was planning to take care of the financial arrangements if they liked it.

The house was far grander than any John had ever imagined he would own. It had a lovely guest bedroom—surely, he thought, his parents would be comfortable on a visit there. Although it was in need of some repair, all in all it was a lovely place. The realtor mentioned that the price was very reasonable, only $85,000. John couldn't believe it. He just wasn't used to thinking in figures like that. Even though his offices were luxurious and the price tag on that space had been staggering, he thought they should consider something less imposing for their first home.

"Really, Joan, it's a bit much. After all, we're just starting; let's look around."

Joan's eyes clouded. He could see she had her heart set on it. "Daddy said we could get new carpet and add on servants' quarters in the back. I love it, John. It's close to the folks and close to the medical center. I don't want to look anywhere else."

They returned to the Robinsons', and when Ash saw his daughter was in a petulant mood, he asked, "What's the matter, honey, didn't you like it?"

"I love it, Daddy. It's just perfect for us. But John thinks we should look for something less expensive."

"Now, John, you're not to worry about that. If Joan likes it, and I know you must like it too, then take it before someone else does. Why, with some new carpet and paint, it could be a real showplace. And there's no question it's a good address."

"I just think we should go a little easy, sir."

"Boy, before you know it, you'll be making more money than you can figure ways to spend. In the meantime, remember appearances count an awful lot. If you look successful, then people will just naturally want to be associated with you. It's like I always tell Joan when she goes to a horse show, 'Look like a winner, honey, and you will be.'

"Now let's see, where's that real estate lady's telephone number. Hello, Ash Robinson here. Well, I think the children want that house you showed them. Dr. Hill has surgery in the morning, so you just send the necessary papers around here to me and I'll take care of it. Fine, thank you."

The new house became a center of activity for all of Joan's crowd. As Ash predicted, John prospered. He decided to add a music room at the back of the house. Although there was a sun room with a piano off the living room wing, John had in mind a more complete salon with room for two pianos. Then he could entertain Julian and their musical friends, and the brothers could again enjoy their piano duets.

As the plan progressed, the music room took on more and more the air of a ballroom. Two years later, when it was completed, it resembled something out of a Louis XIV palace. Everything was white and gold. In addition to the Steinway, John had splurged $15,000 on a custom-made piano. Then there was a built-in projector with a screen that came down from the ceiling at the touch of a switch. The custom-made stereo system was proclaimed by leading authorities in the field the largest residential home entertainment center in the world.

Joan and John traveled to New Orleans to select a pair of matching chandeliers for the room, although at the last minute Joan begged off the shopping expedition and went to a stable to visit friends. Before the furnishings were selected, the cost for the room alone had soared above $200,000.

John spent hours in the music room, planning and measuring, selecting gold brocade for the walls and window coverings. Joan was getting tired of all the interest in what had become known as "John's music room." When it was time to consider a custom-made rug and furniture, she again begged off. "I need to get Robert ready for Post Oak. He's going to compete in the boys' junior division this year. You pick out whatever you want, John."

They had by then developed a routine that kept each of them busy. Joan was as deeply involved with her horse show activities as John was with his medical practice. And now he seemed almost obsessed with his music room.

There had been one unsettling event the previous year. John's brother, Julian, had committed suicide. Julian had spent some time at the Menninger Clinic undergoing psychiatric treatment. The doctors there were concerned about his overdependence on his brother, but when they suggested he might do better in another locale, Julian became suicidal.

Just before his death, Julian had been seeing a good bit of John. They generally met at Julian's apartment since he had never been too comfortable around Joan. When word came one morning that his brother had been found dead, John wasn't too perturbed. If anything, he seemed almost relieved. It was true that poor Julian had never quite found his place in the world, but Joan noticed that John didn't appear greatly upset over the loss of his brother, which struck her as odd since they had always been very close.

A few weeks later, Mr. Hill died. He had had a heart condition for years, and he had been distraught over Julian's death. John took his father's death with total complacency; before he went home for the funeral, he told Joan not to bother making the trip.

By now, John had acquired a polish that belied his small-town origins. He had the easy manner of a man who knows he's a success and savors every moment of it. Music was still the great love of his life; the Hills were patrons of the arts and had box seats at the symphony and the opera. They made contributions to all the charities and appeared at all the right parties, in short, did what was expected of people in their circumstances.

If things wore a little thin around the edges sometimes, well, that was to be expected. After all, it happened to some degree in every marriage, didn't it? Joan was accustomed to John's busy life and she relaxed in the comfortable assurance that she would always enjoy the benefits of being a successful doctor's wife. In any case, she was continually surrounded by her horse-loving friends, so she was just as glad that John had other things to do.

They invariably had houseguests whenever there were horse shows in the vicinity, and frequently John would find Joan and her friends playing bridge when he came in from making hospital rounds. He would peek in the smoke-filled room and say good night. When the occasion called for an appearance, John played the dutiful husband. The Hills tended to entertain in their elegant home, which suited John a lot better than going out to parties.

Actually, they lived in two different worlds, but on the surface it all seemed pleasant enough. Once in a while Joan would drag John to a party, then drink a little too much and get out of hand. On a couple of occasions there had been a minor spat when John had wanted to call it an evening. Joan would refuse to leave, and would then make some disparaging remark about "John wanting to go home to play with his piano, not with his wife, so he could just leave without her." She was always sorry the next day. John seemed to shrug it off.

The summer that Robert was eight, he and his friend from across the street went away to camp. Joan now had all her time to herself, and she practically lived at the farm or at the Robinsons', planning ahead for each horse show. Even though she was getting a little old for it, she found it unthinkable to give up riding, her real love.

John spent more and more time pondering his decisions for the furnishing of the music room. The custom molding and wall covering were being added, and the room was nearly completed. Toward the end of the summer they went to bring Robert home from camp. As they drove toward the hill country, both preoccupied with their own thoughts and interests, neither dreamed of the events that would soon take place to change their lives completely.

ANN

Being on my own again, after my divorce, was beginning to agree with me! My friend Jack Ramsay* and I had spent a glorious afternoon at his ranch, and now we were on our way back to the city—it was time for me to turn back into a mommie. Jack had begged to go with me to Kerrville the next day to take my son Glenn to get his older brothers at camp. However, I thought it would be a bit awkward to have a date since everyone there would be married couples. I was secretly glad when Jack's attempts to find a place to stay were unsuccessful and he was unable to join me. I could hardly wait to see the boys and really wanted some time to be "just our family," so I was unable to sound too disappointed when Jack's last try failed. I was in a rush and promised I'd make it up to him when we got back home in a couple of days. I was very comfortable with our routine but was not at all inclined to get serious.

As we turned into camp that hot August day in 1968, neither my six-year-old son Glenn nor I could have dreamed we were embarking on what would turn out to be the most bizarre episode of our lives.

We had come to collect Mel, twelve, and Jim, eight, at a boys' camp in the hill country of Texas. A divorced mother and three sons, I suppose, were far from being the typical "family" group assembled there.

* Fictitious name.

33

It was just as well Jack wasn't with us. There were hours of "final ceremonies" in the broiling sun—something only a mother could appreciate. It was one of those days that seemed endless!

Before we picked up his brothers, Glenn and I went to the favorite dining place for parents visiting camp. As we waited to be seated, a man struck up a conversation with my little boy.

"What's your name?"

"Glenn."

"Glenn what?"

"Glenn Kurth."

"I'll bet you'll be going to camp next year, Glenn."

"What's your name?"

"Dr. Hill."

"No, it's not!" Glenn teased.

The man chuckled and glanced at me, "Yes, it is! My name is Dr. John Hill."

I laughed and explained. "Glenn goes to Dr. Leighton Hill in Houston. I guess he thinks that's the only Dr. Hill there is."

"Oh! How funny. I know Leighton Hill very well. How old are you, Glenn?"

"Seven, in half a year." Dr. Hill and I smiled, and then I turned away as they called us to our table.

That afternoon at camp, as we made the rounds, it was apparent that Dr. Hill intended to attach himself to our group. The boys took me canoeing, while other parents were attending an archery demonstration. As we lazily paddled down the river, we were overtaken by Dr. Hill. "Hello, Glenn, hi!" He paddled alongside of us. "Are these your brothers?"

"Yes," I answered for him. "This is Mel and Jim. Boys—Dr. Hill."

"Hi," Jim said. "Say, are you Robert Hill's father? He was in my cabin."

"Yes," he smiled. "Robert is my son."

We were friendly but somewhat aloof. Dr. Hill insisted on taking a family picture, but he made the mistake of standing up in his canoe. It was instant disaster! We paddled to shore, and he sloshed right after us, hanging onto his camera, oblivious to the fact that he had totally saturated himself. The boys helped him retrieve his canoe and tie it up.

From then on, Dr. Hill gave every appearance of being part of our family. He completely ignored his wife Joan and son Robert. He later said, "It shows that not only should you send your son to camp, but you shouldn't miss going yourself."

I'm certain a number of people noticed the solicitous doctor, particularly because of all the picture-taking. I asked if he thought he was invisible, and mentioned that his family must surely be looking for him. He indicated that they more or less went their separate ways, and that his wife and son were undoubtedly absorbed with the horse show.

Joan Hill, the doctor's wife, strolled up during a picnic at the end of the day and said, "Hello, Ann." (We had gone to the same girls' school, but I hadn't seen her for several years.) "Isn't this place godawful hot! Hell, now where did John go? I can't seem to keep track of my husband. I want to get out of here. How do you suppose the kids stand it?"

After the final ceremonies at camp, the boys and I went back to our motel, only to find that Dr. Hill and his family were staying in the room next to ours. Glenn and I went for a swim and were joined by a very friendly John Hill. He wanted to know everything about my past, present, and future. I mentioned that I was pretty involved, thinking this would cool him off. But no, he wanted to know what I did all the time, why I was divorced, and why I hadn't married again. I explained that I was happy, and that I dated more than I really wanted to. I tried to get him on the subject of his little boy.

"I scarcely see Robert. He and his mother are in

there now talking about horses. That's their only interest."

I mentioned the fact that I love horses, that Mel had one, and that I had recently taken up riding a cutting horse with a friend, Jack Ramsay.

"I can't see you doing that. You're too sweet and soft and feminine. I know Jack, he's quite the dashing man-about-town. You aren't serious about him, are you? He just doesn't seem your type. Tell me, are you interested in classical music?"

"I can take it or leave it."

"Do you enjoy the symphony and the opera?"

"On occasion, yes."

"Tell me about yourself, Ann."

I told him I was one of those totally programmed young ladies. I was brought up in Houston, went to River Oaks, then Lanier and Lamar, then off to a girl's school. "As a matter of fact, your wife, Joan, was at Stephens when I was, but we seldom saw one another. Then I went to Southern Methodist and faithfully returned home to marry my high school boy friend. My father is an architect, Cameron Fairchild."

"I know him. He designed the Doctors Club in the medical center. He's designed some of the most beautiful homes in River Oaks, I think. Well, I don't actually know him myself, but I certainly know of him," John continued. "Do you have any brothers or sisters?"

"Only sisters. My mother and father always wanted a son, but they had three daughters instead. At least now they have several grandsons. My older sister lives in Arkansas, and my younger sister lived in Kansas until she and her husband were killed in a plane crash just four months ago."

"I'm so sorry to hear that. I know what is it to be close to a brother or sister and lose them. I came from a family of three. I have a sister—my brother, whom I was very close to, died a couple of years ago. But go on, don't let me barge in. What happened to your marriage—were you married long?"

"Yes," I said. "I was. I was married to Melvin Kurth for nearly fourteen years. We just grew apart, I guess. We lived in East Texas for several years, then the boys and I moved back to Houston a couple of years ago, and we were divorced. After that, I married again, briefly, and ever since that was over I have been so glad to be on my own, I haven't wanted to be involved with anyone."

"You just weren't married to the right person," John said. "You're supposed to love being married and love being together. At least, that's the way it *should* be. Not that I'm speaking from personal experience. Sometimes I wonder if any two people can really be happy together forevermore." John looked at me intently, "I'm certain I remember you from someplace. I've been trying all afternoon to place you. Where do you live now?"

"Way out in Memorial," I told him.

"That can't be it. We live on Kirby Drive."

"Well, I grew up just a block off Kirby, but that was a number of years ago."

"Did you ever work at the Junior League clinic at Herman Hospital?"

"Why, yes—about twelve years ago."

"I remember! That's it! You used to be there on Wednesdays, right? I was just a struggling intern, but I sure remember you! Why haven't I seen you since?"

"Because we moved to East Texas. The boys and I haven't been back in Houston that long, and I just never had time to go back to my League work." Glenn ran up to me, shivering. It was late, so I dried off my little boy, and said good night.

The next morning the boys and I returned to Houston. The phone was ringing as I walked into the house. It was John. He wanted to come by for a cup of coffee that evening to show us the pictures he had taken of us at camp.

He came and stayed.

And stayed.

I was exhausted when he left. I finally got to sleep, and it seemed only minutes later that the phone rang. Actually, it was 6 A.M. John was getting ready to begin surgery and had called to say how much he enjoyed his visit. He wanted to know what plans I had for the day.

"I'll probably be unpacking the boys' trunks all *week,*" I told him.

I went back to sleep and he called again between operations. While we were talking, the doorbell rang. John told me to see who it was, that he'd hang on. When I reported it was just a family friend, he quickly said, "Don't make any plans, you're having lunch with me." When I returned from our lunch, I found a beautiful bouquet of flowers and a note from John (the first of hundreds of such thoughtful gestures).

That afternoon I went to the beauty shop; John called me there to see what time I'd be finished, and he was waiting when I got out. He suggested he would follow me home, then we could go out to dinner. I explained that my parents were coming over but said he could come by for a drink.

John got into his car, which was in back of mine. Just as I was about to pull out into traffic, I saw Jack Ramsay driving by. When Jack spotted me, he double-parked beside me and got out of his car. "I've called you all day," he said. "Didn't the maid tell you to call?" I explained that I'd been busy, and that my parents were coming to dinner and I had to dash. Jack leaned in the car window, gave me a kiss, and said he would call the next day.

When I got to the next stoplight, a little boy knocked on my window and offered me a bunch of Tyler roses. "No thanks," I said.

"They're for you, lady—from the man in that car."
I looked back and saw Jack waving.

When I got home, John took the little bunch of roses
out of my hand and said, "You don't need those—and
you don't need him!"

I had a hard time convincing John to leave so I
could finish getting dinner ready. I was delighted to
have the boys home; I had hardly seen them, so
after dinner, my parents and I took them to the pool
where they could show us their diving and swimming.
By nine o'clock, we were all ready to call it a day. But
as soon as my parents left, John pulled in the driveway. We had another long visit, and as our conversation continued, I realized I had never before talked
so freely about myself or my feelings to a person I
scarcely knew. I wondered why he was asking so
many questions.

"You make me feel like you're auditioning me or
something," I complained. "You will never know another person who is so uninterested in getting involved,
much less seriously. I have very definite plans to spend
the next several years enjoying my boys. Even dating
interferes more than I like."

John chuckled. "I guess I really have been overly
inquisitive. I think I became fascinated by you years
ago when I used to see you at the clinic. You realize,
don't you, that you have a very aloof attitude? But
what I find most intriguing is just watching you with
your boys. I've never seen a family that seemed to
have such obvious devotion. But that's not quite it,
either. There's just something about you. I can't put
my finger on it. A presence, an effervescence, something
indescribable that draws me to you."

"Don't get carried away," I said. "Whatever you
may think, I'm an ordinary person who plans to remain exactly as I am, where I am; I have no interest
in being attached to someone else. I guess I have a
sort of built-in defense mechanism that keeps me from

being interested in anyone else. I have become accustomed to being totally in charge of my family. I don't think I could change back to being a submissive wife if I had to. Actually, for me it's easier to make all the decisions, to be the first and last word on the way the boys and I lead our lives. In short, I'm alone by choice and I like it this way. Anyone who has been through two disappointing marriages followed by the trauma of two divorces would understand my feeling." I laughed. "I really *do* have my life just exactly the way I want it."

"Don't say that. Don't close any doors. Wait till we get to know each other better. You'll find I'm not like anyone you've ever known. Just be a little patient. And a little understanding. Just give yourself a chance to see that there's a kind of person in this world that you never knew existed. Then maybe you'll decide to let me in your world.

"I'm glad I found you again," he went on. "I hate to sound so foolish, but you must have noticed, when I used to see you at the clinic on Wednesdays, that I was fascinated by you. I remember you were planning to go to Europe that summer. Then you never came back."

"That's right, I did go to Europe for the summer with my sister-in-law. Then my husband changed jobs, and we moved to East Texas the day after I got home. You really do have a memory."

"Ann, please bear with me. Joan is leaving for a horse show in a few days. We seldom see each other. Our relationship is nothing more now than a legal formality. But I can't go on like that anymore. It's a pointless existence. I'm going to talk to an attorney and find out the best way to terminate my marriage. Actually a lot of people wondered why Joan and I remain married. We were at a party not too long ago and had a most unpleasant scene. After I left the party alone, an attorney who overheard the fight told a friend of mine that he would be glad to represent me when I decided I'd had enough. I think I'll give him a call. I don't want to rush you," he went on, "but I don't want to lose you either. I know you are dating Jack. Could you please just put him off a little while, and let me have the chance to really get to know you. Hopefully you will come to know me and maybe even love me. I have such an overwhelming desire to be with you. After you and Glenn went in the other evening at camp, I thought about you all night, and you are all I have been able to think about since then.

"I know I'm way ahead of you," he said, "but all I ask is that you give me a chance, and let us get to know each other. Without any interruptions."

"John, I really don't want you to feel that way about me. What you are saying is awfully sweet, but I think I've developed an allergy to being involved with anyone. I want to be my own self. I want to live a happy uncluttered life. I don't want to get caught up in all those games people play."

"No games, I promise you. In fact, nothing you don't want will be thrust upon you. If you honestly get tired or bored with me, just say so. I will abide by your wishes. Just give me some time to show you."

"But you *are* married, and you must be very busy with your work."

"There's nothing as important to me as a sense of completeness and that's something I don't have. I never even felt an inkling of it until the other night when I stayed awake for hours thinking about you. From thinking about you, I went on to thinking about you with me, and me with you and your little family. I watched you and your boys all day at camp. Robert and I have nothing in common. He's close to his mother and they both think of nothing but their horses. I've never wanted anything so much in my life as I want to be part of a family like yours.

"It's something I've never had. It's something I've

never even seen before. I've always kept myself content and busy with my medical practice. My great love has been music. I could always take out my frustrations playing the piano. Sometimes I get up at night and play for hours."

"I didn't know you played the piano, John."

"You don't know anything about me; nothing, in fact, but what I've told you. I want you to be with me and see for yourself. See if I can't show you what I think we can be together."

It was an overwhelming conversation, and I admit I was flattered. John was a very unusual person; he was terribly polite and solicitous, very appealing in every way. But I had become so accustomed to leading my own life, calling all the plays, that I couldn't just turn loose and let someone else take the lead. I didn't even want to think about getting involved with someone. And yet, John was more than slightly convincing. After all, when someone is saying those flattering things we all want to hear about ourselves (no matter how deep inside we bury the craving), it's hard not to think favorably of them.

He was certainly charming enough. And when he looked at me with those deep blue eyes . . . those eyes made love to me whenever he looked at me. Maybe it would be best to let him see for himself; probably he would find we had less in common than he imagined.

Up to this point we hadn't been on the same wavelength. John had been watching me and conjuring up no telling what in his mind. Even years before, he had been watching me. I now vaguely recalled a pleasant medical student from the clinic, but the memory was not very clear. He, on the other hand, had attached great importance to everything.

"John, please don't make me feel like I am on a stage. Don't watch me and make me sense your eyes on me all the time," I said.

"Don't let me make you feel awkward." John put his arm around me and smiled. I wasn't prepared for that, nor for any physical contact. I had very strong defenses that prevented such casual closeness with a man I scarcely knew. I rose quickly and got some more coffee from the kitchen.

"All right, John. We'll be friends, but remember, I want to be *me!* And I've *got* to get some sleep. So here's just enough coffee to keep you awake till you get home. You must be exhausted, too."

"Not really. I could stay here talking to you for hours if you'd let me. But I'll go now and leave you to think about everything I've said. Maybe you'll even find yourself thinking about me. Please do! Good night, Ann." And he gave me a kiss on the cheek and left.

Within two weeks he filed for divorce, moved to an apartment, and we became inseparable.

All during September of 1968 John would call from surgery and talk for hours while a nurse held the phone to his ear. He always had his stereo on in the background, playing his favorite Rachmaninoff or Mozart.

I begged him not to call and leave his name at my parents' house or the beauty shop, or wherever I might be when I was away from home. "I'll just say it's *Mr. Hyde,*" he said, "then you'll know it's me."

"Like Dr. Jekyll and Mr. Hyde?"

"Exactly. J. R. Hyde, instead of John R. Hill."

I laughed and wondered what I was going to do about him. Meanwhile I had put Jack Ramsay off so much that finally I just had to tell him I needed "time out." He was nice, though a bit hurt, and asked me to let me know when the intermission was over.

Although all the affection and attention from John certainly made an impression on me, I never told him I loved him. This put him on edge and he set out trying in every conceivable way to win my love. Finally, he blurted out, "Don't you love me? Please, please, tell me you love me." I told him I would tell him when I did.

This made him frantic. He immediately canceled his appointments for the next few days and took me to San Antonio so there would be no interruption in his pursuit, which was rapidly becoming an obsession. He refused to take me home until I finally told him I loved him. By then I had learned to unwind and enjoy the pleasure of having him surround me with his love. Happily calmed, he proceeded to plan our lives together. I was glad to see he seemed to enjoy being with the boys and included them in all his plans for us as a happy family.

John was the most fascinating person I had ever known. Without being conscious of exactly how and when, he had drawn me to him in a way I had never thought possible. He soon had my every moment happily occupied. I had never known a man so filled with tenderness and love who still remained strong and compelling. Sometimes I wondered if he had hypnotized me. By then I was completely under his spell, and deeply in love—never mind how he had achieved it!

Even though I had taken such a stand against becoming involved, I found it impossible to refuse John's persistent appeal to give it a chance. Once I became accustomed to having him so completely in my life, I knew I couldn't be happy without him. He soon convinced me that together our lives would hold more than I had ever known with another man. To be alone after I grew to love John would have meant an emptiness I couldn't bear.

He was right. We did belong together. Although I was at first reluctant to admit it, I soon realized how very much I craved his love. Because of my previous disappointments, I had simply given up and become resigned to a life alone. Now I knew he was right to insist that I give him a chance to prove we belonged together. This was one time in my life that I was glad to find out I had been wrong. Together everything was happier. Everything shared became all the more savored. Once I allowed it to flourish, all the love I had been keeping hidden within myself was all the more intense for having been denied so long.

Together we were so perfectly in tune. I was surprised to find there really was a person I could feel so comfortable with. I never wanted to be alone again. The children were delighted to see their mother so radiantly happy. When I looked in the mirror I knew there was no better beauty treatment than falling completely in love.

As we explored the depths of our feelings for one another, we became oblivious to the past each of us had known. There was no reason to ever be apart. There was no question about what we each wanted. That we were together was all that mattered. Both of us were glad to sense that the only thing either of us wanted was each other.

Once this happy state was reached, there were no questions, no uncertainties. We were one, we felt no pressures. We knew no problems. We had each other, and both of us were completely committed and fulfilled by our love.

When we were together tenderly, lovingly, the effect was so strong, so complete that the afterglow never diminished. To touch him, to feel his hand was to make love. To hear his voice was to hear my thoughts put in words. To look into his eyes was to see the depth of our love reflected there.

He was the man I never had believed existed. What a pathetic excuse the others had been. How wonderful to be the recipient of such a love. He made me a warmer, happier, more complete woman than I had ever been.

During October and November, John and I went to the symphony and to the opera. The gossip columns were buzzing with comments—"John and Joan Hill are telling it to the judge." I kept warning John that he wasn't invisible, but if the truth be known, he just didn't care. We went to parties and out to dinner, oblivious to all the world around us. We spent a lot of time with the boys, and John insisted on getting to know my parents. Everyone got along well and we were all very happy. The time for his divorce, which he assured me was merely a formality, was close at hand.

John would write out silly prescriptions for me, always calling for large doses of HIM. You can use your own imagination about the medical terms: to be taken internally, twice a day, as directed by physician.

I was given a paging device so that John could reach me anywhere when we weren't together. "I'm going to surround you completely with my love," John told me. "When I leave you for a while, you can always reach me, and I must always be able to reach you. But most of all, our love will be so strong that no matter how much time or distance separates us, you will always feel my presence and love. I want you to be so content and so complete there will never be an unhappy moment for you from this time on! I have to have you. Nobody can stop me. Promise you won't ever try to leave me. That would just push me over the edge."

He was right. I did feel totally complete (not that I had ever felt *in*complete before). I guess there's no way to explain chemistry. And even if there were, it wouldn't have done me any good. Maybe it had something to do with destiny. Maybe it was true when he said, "You are the rest of me, and I am the rest of you, the beginning and the end."

We had no conflicts, no upsets, no doubts, nothing but a perfect relationship. Each seemed to know what the other was thinking, and we would laugh whenever we said something at the same time, which was often.

John was so enthusiastic about life, particularly our lives together, that it was truly contagious.

I soon grew to feel as if whatever might have been missing in my life before, even though I hadn't consciously missed anything, was all there now. Sometimes I think about the way we were that fall. I would have to count it the prime time of my life. I felt a kind of self-assurance and inner glow, a reflection of the way John affected me.

I already had a beautiful home, and the boys and I were very well provided for. John was very interested in the "boys' music" and spent hours setting up amps and speakers—and he was great about taking them places and hauling their motorbikes around. He would often stand and watch them, just as proud as if he'd taught them everything himself.

John was forever trying to make thoughtful gestures and constantly sent flowers addressed to "The beautifulest mommie in the world." He was fond of that quote and frequently addressed his cards to me that way. When Glenn would see us being affectionate with each other, he would come up, put his little arms around us, and look at John and say, "Isn't she the beautifulest mommie in the world!" Happiness *is* contagious!

John was thrilled over what to us were trivial things that we had always enjoyed together, like the flowers and the fountain in the garden, the music throughout the house, and the various "family customs." Every day seemed to be a special event to John.

Once he started complaining about Joan, commenting on her forcefulness and the fact that she smoked incessantly. He detested cigarette smoke, and he said he was sick of a wife who smelled like a goat. He said she used to humiliate him at parties and that she was very unfeminine. "She walks and talks like a man. She's crude and domineering and loves to tell dirty jokes wherever she is. Her voice grates in my ears, and our den looks like a tackroom."

I told him not to think for a minute that if Joan were so bad I would ever want *her leftovers*. He was deeply resentful of her and her father and their constant preoccupation with show horses. Their obsession with horses had made it easy for him to feel totally apart from their world.

His world was music and his medical practice, and his Shangri-La was the palatial music room he had added to their home. He even had a piano in a lovely salon at his office where he would have a cup of tea and discuss forthcoming surgery with his patients in an atmosphere designed to make them feel pampered. Surely this was a little out of the ordinary for a plastic surgeon!

Joan and her father, Ash Robinson, were incensed by John's abrupt departure and hired a detective to find out about the "other woman," meanwhile denying the possibility that there would be a divorce, ever! This hardly fit into John's plans. He had intended to move Joan and Robert into a nice but smaller home and establish his new family in the River Oaks mansion, where we would live happily ever after in "opulent splendor," as he put it.

However, John became alarmed when he noticed someone following him. Soon I discovered that someone was following me wherever I went. It was unsettling, but John didn't quite know what to do about it.

One day a friend of Jim's at school asked him to spell his last name. "K-U-R-T-H."

"Is your mother named Ann?"

"Yes," Jim answered. "Why, do you know my mom?"

"No, but my father is a private detective. He's working on a case watching her for Ash Robinson."

That evening Jim asked John if he knew Ash Robinson.

"Why, yes, Jim—that's Joan's father—Robert's grandfather. Why do you ask?"

When Jim repeated his school friend's comment, John was furious at his father-in-law.

Then Joan called one day and said, "Is this Ann Kurth? Ann, this is Joan Robinson Hill."

"Yes, Joan."

"I'd like to know just exactly what is going on with you and John. My father has had a detective watching you. He tells me you live in Memorial, and that you are divorced and have *three* sons. Is that right?"

"Yes, that's correct," I answered.

"I'll bet John doesn't know that. We have a son, and he certainly isn't very interested in children. If you don't mind my asking, just how and where did you and John meet?"

"At camp, when we were all there in August collecting our boys. I saw you there, too; remember, Joan?"

There was a long pause. Then Joan blurted: "Good Lord! Is this Ann Fairchild?" She used my maiden name.

"Yes," I said quietly.

"Oh, my God. I had no idea it was you. Well, I really don't know what to say. I thought John was just off on a fling. After he had been gone several weeks, Daddy hired a private detective to check on him. That's how I got your name and number, but I didn't realize it was you.

"Well," she continued, "I know John and I have become distant, but now he says he wants a divorce. In fact, I just found out he filed for a divorce about six weeks ago. I've been off at a horse show the past couple of weeks, and I guess I just figured we'd work it out when I got back. But I can't get him to talk to me. I mean—well, uh, are you all *serious,* or is it just a fling, or what?"

"Joan, I really think it would be better for you to talk all this over with John."

"I wish I knew how I could. I don't even know where his apartment is, and his telephone is unlisted. I haven't seen him in over a month. I guess I'm just going to have to let Daddy get a lawyer if John is really serious about this divorce thing. There's no way he'll ever get a divorce from me."

I knew she was upset, and I certainly couldn't blame her.

"I've called his office, and left messages," she continued, "but John won't even talk to me on the phone. Poor Robert never sees his father, and I've been gone so much. If it weren't for my parents, he wouldn't have any family at all. Well," she sighed, "I'm sorry I called so mad."

"Joan, I really do understand. I think John should talk it over with you; I agree he ought to spend time with Robert. I guess it's awkward, but I will make that suggestion to him," I said.

She was very nice then, most appreciative, and said, "We wouldn't have any problems if John were half as nice to me as you've been. Thank you, Ann; good-bye."

As I was hanging up, John walked in. He was furious that Joan had called me. We had a long conversation, and I told him it was all wrong to expect that Joan would ever understand or that things would be all right when he wouldn't even discuss the situation with her.

A few weeks later Ash Robinson called John at his office and told him that "his little world" was soon going to come to an end; he added that if he didn't get over to his house at eight that night, he needn't expect to see Robert ever again. And further, he would see to it that his "girl friend" would be the object of so much gossip and scandal that she would "never be able to hold her head up in society."

As if to punctuate the terse message my doorbell rang with a summons for me to appear to have a deposition taken in a cross action Joan had filed against John, naming me. Later, the children came in, pale with fear, and said Joan was following Glenn on his bicycle down the boulevard. John jumped in his car and went down the block. He found Glenn, with Joan driving beside him just looking at him, and he shepherded the boy home. Once home, John picked up the phone and called Ash to tell them to keep away. Ash said John had better be at his house by eight that night, or he would be facing very dire consequences not only for himself but for me and my children as well.

When John had the meeting that night with Ash and Joan, he was told he would never get a divorce, much less the house (on which Joan's father had made the down payment, Ash chastised John for being interested in finding a high society girl friend, one who probably enjoyed his long-hair music and who could introduce him into the Junior League group. Ash had done quite a bit of research on the subject of John's "girl friend" and he bitterly denounced him for leaving the good life and the good wife he had furnished him, to "step up on the social ladder."

There were several broad hints that the irate Mr. Robinson had Mafia connections he wouldn't hesitate to use unless the romance ended immediately and John returned to his home. John was given an ultimatum. He signed a letter, written by Ash Robinson, to the effect that he would make a substantial cash settlement with Joan immediately, and that should a separation occur later, Joan would receive the house and large sums of money. Since all of this would serve to cancel the divorce action and my deposition slated for the next day, John was glad to sign it. He would find another way to terminate the marriage.

The letter, written on the personal stationery of Ash Robinson and dictated by him, went as follows:

December 9, 1968

Dear Joan,

I ask that you become reconciled with me and forgive me my transgressions. I will come back home and be a good husband to you and a good father to Robert.

In the event of any future separation for whatever reason I will:

Deed the house at 1561 Kirby to you.

Pay off all remaining indebtedness along with taxes, insurance, and upkeep.

I will take out a life insurance policy to pay off the home mortgage in case of my death.

I will provide you with $1,000 a month for household and personal expenses.

I will place in your bank account $7,000 immediately.

John

John later referred to this document as "Joan's death certificate, authored by her own father."

While he pacified his irate father-in-law by spending time on the home front with his wife and son on a more regular basis, John still stayed with his "new family" as much as possible. He fiercely resented any "command performances" he was called on to make by Joan or her father, and he became more and more bitter toward them, and certainly more determined to carry out his plan to terminate his marriage.

During this period, John became quite intense about everything. He took a lot of pills (what they were, I had no idea) and often stayed awake for two days and nights at a time. He was always on the go, and would call or drop by my house at any hour. Every time he went to his house to put in an appearance, he arranged for his answering service to call him in a few minutes, saying he had to go to the emergency room, so that he could leave. He became so accustomed to this deception that sometimes we would be sitting in my living room and his paging device would sound; he would call his answering service and only then remember that he really *had* been called to the hospital, and they were wondering why he hadn't shown up.

His biggest concern was that I would grow tired of the situation. The thought that we might lose what we had together haunted him. He was determined to keep my mind and heart and body completely his. He remained in constant contact and continually made plans with me and the boys. We all went to the motorcycle races at the Astrodome and to the circus and other such inconspicuous places. With time, the smoke seemed to clear, but I wondered at John's nerve when he was with us so much. John maintained that he and Joan had had separate interests for a long time and that she wasn't used to seeing much of him anyway. In any case she was busy with horse shows and trips with friends.

Over the Christmas holidays John took a room at a nearby motel, under the name of J. R. Hyde, in case Joan was checking on his apartment. When I was alone, he urged me to be cautious, saying Joan and Ash were both quite vindictive. Since they had had both of us followed, he wanted to be certain they never again upset me or the children. He got a gun for me; he told me to keep it safely hidden from the boys, but to have it handy to protect myself in the event Ash or Joan ever took further action against me, as Ash had promised he would do.

At Christmas, John was like a child in a toy store, shopping for the boys. I think he had missed a lot of the presents and festivities that many children associate with Christmas, and he was determined to get one of everything he saw for each boy. As is often the case, he had more fun playing with everything than the children did. He was there Christmas morning when the boys woke up. He dashed to dinner at the Robinsons, then came right back to play with the boys and their Christmas toys, and that night we went out together.

In fact, we were together all the time, except for brief appearances at his home. The divorce action and cross action had been dropped when he signed the letter authored by Ash, and he now had the task of trying to talk Joan into *please* giving him a divorce.

He was certain he could calmly and pleasantly talk her into terminating their marriage. He felt he could convince her it was pointless to continue. John had gotten very nervy about calling me, even when he went by his and Joan's house to check on the continuing construction of the music room. Sometimes he would even call when she was in the room: "Mrs. Hyde, how are you? Just wanted to tell you I should be through here in about twenty minutes and I will be there." Then he would whisper: "I love you, baby!"

Joan must have known what he was up to, but I think at this point she believed that time would solve the problem. John, on the other hand, seemed to feel that time apart, for us, was a terrible enemy. He said there could have been no worse punishment than the time he spent with Joan.

One night in January, while John was with me, I had a call from Jack Ramsay. We chatted a minute, then Jack said, "Say, I gather it's all off with you and John. Why don't we take the boys and go to the ranch this weekend?" I told him I had plans. Then he said, "I saw Joan at a party without John last night and she was laughing about how she and her father had really 'fixed him'; she said that John had had to pay her a small fortune and make all kinds of promises 'to be a good boy,' etc., etc." I got off the phone as quickly as I could and repeated to John what Jack had told me. John was *livid! "That does it!* I've tried every way I know to be nice about this in hopes that she would see I could never care for her. She *knows* I love you. I've *told* her so. Why in the world she wants to ridicule me at parties, then do everything in the world she and her father can think of to hang on is more than I can figure! But I'm through. That just settles it. She's asking for it, and I'll get the last laugh." He didn't go back to their house for several days.

A few mornings later, as I was going to a nearby shopping center, I noticed Joan behind me in traffic. I ran a couple of errands, then went to try on a dress I'd seen a few days before. As I came out of the dressing room and walked to a full-length mirror, I saw Joan standing there, as if waiting for me. I glanced in the mirror, and Joan said, "Hello." At that moment my paging device, which I had left in my purse in the dressing area, buzzed. I dashed to turn it off, and gave Joan plenty of time to leave the store before I reemerged from the fitting room.

In February, there was to be a gala ball honoring the famous heart surgeons from Houston. I was invited to attend by Jack. Although I hadn't seen him again, he had called from time to time. John was totally distraught over the invitation. Just a few days before the ball, he took me to his office one Sunday and performed minor surgery on my eyelids, assuring me that it was a simple procedure. (It was an upper blepharoplasty.) Simple, yes, but my eyes and face were swollen and black and blue for about ten days. Naturally, that precluded any possibility of my going to the heart ball— with anyone!

On Valentine's Day I received a bouquet of roses with a card that read:

When?
Jack

Later the florist delivered a beautiful basket of spring flowers from John. When he came over to dinner that evening and saw the roses Jack had sent, he was terribly upset. I tried to assure him that there was nothing at all to it, but he was afraid there soon would be. Nonetheless we had a happy dinner with the boys and exchanged silly Valentines. John had brought each of the boys and me boxes of candy. We had tiny heart-shaped cakes for dessert, and John was just like a little boy who had never been to a Valentine party before. He was clearly touched by the dinner and the party atmosphere.

He poured each of us a glass of wine and made a toast "to the happiest family in the world, forever and ever." He said we were to forget the past and concentrate only on our happy life together. He told me he was going to have a businesslike meeting with Joan and Ash, and after that, there would be no more problems or unpleasant encounters. The situation with Joan was totally changed, he said. She was about to give in to a divorce, and it would be very soon—and on *his* terms.

You can't spend as much time together as John and I did without getting to feel as though you are a part of one another. We were both delighted by the direction in which our life together was moving. Except for the upheavals with Joan and her father, we had no problems, other than finding enough time to enjoy each other. Sometimes I was a bit concerned about the amount of time John spent away from his patients, but he assured me that we needed each other more than his patients needed him.

At one point, there were two medical conventions on his agenda, the first in New York and the other in Mexico. He missed his scheduled plane to New York— he just couldn't say good-bye. When he got there later, he phoned often and talked on more than one occasion for an hour at a time. In Mexico he just left the convention—he didn't stay to read his paper as scheduled —and came back two days early. He seemed quite keyed up about everything, and very happy.

One day in early March we stopped by his apartment. As I went into the bathroom, John came up behind me and quickly said, "Don't go in there, darling. I'm doing an experiment." I caught a glimpse of a goose-neck lamp turned on over three containers that looked like plastic cheese dishes (I later learned they are called Petri dishes) which held something bright red with whitish dots on top.

A little later, while John was busy going through some papers, I went into the kitchen to get a snack. I found a box of pastries in the refrigerator and called out: "John, which kind of pastry do you want? And why did you get blueberry? You know I hate blueberries!" A very flustered John rushed in, put the pastries back in the refrigerator, and said, "Let's don't have those, I'm hungry for Mexican food," and with that, he steered me out to dinner.

On another occasion, when we were making hospital rounds one evening, I phoned home, only to find that Glenn had taken some of my pills by accident. John spoke on the phone to Mel and got a description of the pills Glenn had taken. We rushed to a pharmacy. Since John was dictating medical notes on the portable tape machine he kept in his car, he asked me to run in and get a bottle of ipecac.

When the pharmacist told me I needed a prescription, I went to the car and asked John for one. Instead of writing a prescription, he simply said, "Oh, well, we'll just get it at Herman Hospital. Glenn really should get those pills out of his system—and this will make him throw them up."

When I reminded John that Glenn is a diabetic and takes insulin, that he needs to have a balance of food and insulin, and that he gets out of control if he throws up, he just said, "I'm the doctor, remember? I know what I'm doing."

The pharmacy was closed by the time we got to Herman, so John drove to St. Luke's Hospital. Since he was once again dictating medical notes, he asked me to go to the pharmacy and tell the pharmacist that my little boy had gotten into my pills; he would be glad to give me the ipecac, according to John. And as it turned out, he was, although I did have to sign for the drug. John then stopped at a service station and got some Cokes, despite my insistence that I had a whole case at home.

We stopped by John's apartment where he called Mel and found that Glenn had apparently suffered no ill effects from the pills. After all the trouble we had gone to getting a remedy for Glenn's pill-taking, John then decided that Glenn was fine and that we should just stay at the apartment for a while. When we finally got to my house, we both checked and found Glenn sleeping peacefully.

I went to sleep, and, as usual, John called early in the morning from surgery. When I asked what to do about Glenn, he said, "Forget it, he's fine. Oh, I took the ipecac and Cokes. You might get some to keep on hand for an emergency, though." That's the last I thought of that, for a time.

On Tuesday, March 18, 1969, I met John after he had played at a school concert; we had planned to go out for coffee and donuts. Joan had had houseguests, and I had seen less of John than usual the previous weekend. He came out from the concert, looking pre-occupied, and said he couldn't make it for coffee after all. Joan was sick with a bug, and he had to go check on her. I asked if he had noticed in the paper that the exterminator who parked next to him at his apartment parking lot had been found dead in his apartment under mysterious circumstances? John's only comment was "Really?"

I then said I didn't think he should be so careless about not locking his door, to which he responded, "Don't you ever worry about me. Remember, I'm going to live with you happily ever after, and *nobody* can stop me. Look, baby, real soon we are going to be together all the time—I promise you—and no one can interfere with that." He mentioned some plans he had with the boys, gave me a kiss, and said he would call and see me shortly.

But he didn't call while I was home. The maid said my private phone (the one just for John) rang, but she didn't get to it in time. That night, when John hadn't called or showed up, I was bewildered, but I stayed busy with the boys. In any event, I had a friend coming to visit from Dallas the next day, so I was somewhat preoccupied.

The next morning, while I was out doing some shopping, my paging device sounded. When I called home, the maid said that she had been in the kitchen so if Dr. Hill had called, she hadn't heard, but that I had had a call earlier from a friend, Lu, and I was to call her at the beauty parlor; I had also had a call from my stockbroker.

Both had called for the same reason: "Have you heard? Joan Hill died!" I couldn't believe it. They knew no details, but said it was on the news. Lu told me that everybody at the beauty parlor was talking about it. I just couldn't believe it!

When I got home, I turned on the news, and there it was: pictures and a story about the sudden death of noted horsewoman Joan Robinson Hill. She had reportedly died of pancreatitis. I was sure John would call. Everyone else did. Then the papers came, full of the story.

My friend Joyce from Dallas arrived, eager to meet John—she had heard so much about him—and instead found me in a state of shock. By then the news reports said Joan had had hepatitis. I was certain that that was why John hadn't called. He must have hepatitis too. (Would I get it, I wondered.) I was desperate to talk to John and make sure he was all right. Joyce and I went to see Lu, the girl who had called me earlier that day. Both of them tried to calm me, pointing out that if John weren't okay, he would know what to do; after all, he was a doctor.

The papers and television reports were filled with details about the funeral. I knew John was undoubtedly surrounded by family and friends, and that he also had to be with his little boy.

Finally, after several days that seemed like ages, John called. He sounded awful. He said he had to see me. There was still lots of family around, but he was going to take Robert to a movie and he wanted me to meet him at the shopping center.

I was shocked when we met. He looked terrible. It was a dark, dreary day, yet he had on sunglasses.

He got in my car and slumped in the seat. I was alarmed at his voice and his appearance, and asked him to take off the sunglasses. He looked at me strangely.

He said, "I've got to tell you that Joan . . ."

"No," I said, "please don't. I'm worried about you. You're going to be sick, if you aren't already."

"Well," he said. "I just wanted you to know that Joan . . ."

"No, please leave whatever was between you and Joan in the past. Please don't give me a lot of details and make a monument to the situation."

"I'm so glad it's all over, I just wanted to say that Joan looked better in her coffin than I ever saw her."

He seemed to relax somewhat after this strange comment. I let the remark pass, and asked about Robert. John said his mother was taking care of Robert and that he wanted me to meet her. I assured him I would, at some more appropriate time. He really didn't seem to be thinking too clearly, and I was concerned most of all about how terrible he looked.

On the Sunday following Joan's funeral, John went to church with his mother. He later said that he had "gone down and confessed all my sins, before the congregation—no details, just in general. Everyone was so nice afterwards, and came up and congratulated me. I feel so much better—being saved."

From then on, when we were together, there were

only scant references made to Joan's "passing," as he put it. He tried to spend some time with Robert, who was nervous and upset.

A grand jury was considering Joan Hill's sudden death, and I was called before them to answer some of their questions. They wanted to know what Dr. Hill had told me concerning Joan's illness, and I answered truthfully, that we seldom discussed Joan. They had called all the attending doctors in order to determine why her health had deteriorated so rapidly and whether or not the medical attention she received had been adequate. John was sure Ash Robinson was trying to make him to look negligent in treating Joan.

About a month after Joan's death, I took a little dish garden with tiny fish and turtles by John's house for Robert. He was at school, but I visited with John's mother for a minute. She was a strange, austere woman. John had already told me she was quite a religious fanatic. The meeting was pleasant, and when John came home, she gave a glowing report about the lovely lady who had brought such a nice gift to Robert. According to John, she urged him to become interested in someone like that and forget all about Joan and Ash and their kind. (John had, of course, long since done just that and more!)

A week or so later, at John's insistence, I asked Mrs. Hill to lunch. We got along well, even though she seemed rather stern and sprinkled her conversation liberally with misquoted Bible verses. Mrs. Hill was obviously *glad* Joan was dead. At one point she went on about how hateful Joan was to her and that until now she had never been comfortable in John's house. She stated authoritatively, "Joan's death was an act of God."

Mrs. Hill said she knew all along that John should *never* have married Joan. She told me that a few days before the wedding, she and Mr. Hill had received an anonymous letter with a picture of Ash Robinson in a striped prison suit. The letter described the Robinsons as "unscrupulous people who were trying to find a respectable husband for a daughter who had a fast reputation and had already been married twice before." The anonymous author went on to say that they knew John came from a fine Christian family, and the Hills shouldn't allow their son to be bought by "a crook who has been to the penitentiary for stealing maps from an oil company." She was quite bitter that John had disregarded their advice years ago and had discounted the letter as the product of someone who was jealous of Joan and her success at horse shows.

I mentioned this conversation to John. He said as it turned out, it was all quite true. Joan had told him about the time when she was very young and Ash was away. Then, she told him, there was a reversal of the conviction due to a technicality (they had his name spelled wrong or something), and he was released.

Joan had been adopted, John continued; when she was grown, she was contacted once after a horse show by a woman who claimed to be her real mother. John said she had found the visit very upsetting. The woman, whom Joan indeed resembled, was a waitress in a small-town bus station restaurant. She told Joan she had had a brief affair with Ash Robinson, only to find herself pregnant afterwards. She contacted Mr. Robinson, who at first would not help her in any way. Then he got back in touch with her and said he and his wife would adopt the baby. She agreed, realizing they could give her little girl all sorts of advantages.

Joan never tried to see her mother again. The Robinsons had been the only family she had ever known, and Ash, after all, *was* her real father. How sad for Joan. I admired her for being able to digest all this unwelcome news and go on to conduct her life in a busy, happy way.

John said Ash had always controlled Joan. Before she married John, Ash had been instrumental in breaking up her two previous marriages. The first, when she was quite young, was annulled; and Ash had had her get a divorce from her second husband. He wanted her to concentrate on a more respectable life, one in which she could feel at ease in River Oaks, among the rich elite of Houston.

After Joan's death, John concentrated his attention on Robert, trying to keep him happy. The two had never been close, and Robert scarcely knew his grandmother Hill, who was now taking care of him, so there were many difficult days. To make matters worse, John decided that since Ash and Rhea Robinson weren't exactly favorites of his mother's, this would be as good a time as any to let them know they couldn't control Robert's life as they had Joan's. So Robert seldom saw the Robinsons unless they drove by while he was playing outside.

Myra Hill told Robert that his grandfather was a "heathen and an ex-convict, and if he knew what was good for him he would study his Bible and live a righteous life." She refused to let him go to visit his grandparents, even though they lived in the next block. Poor Robert missed his mother, and now his grandparents, who had practically raised him, were unwelcome. These were not happy days for him.

One evening in April John and I went to dinner at a quiet little restaurant in my neighborhood. I felt we should have dinner at my house since Joan had recently died, and after all, John had been married to her, even though they were separated. But John said that was ridiculous, and insisted we go to our favorite steak place. After we were seated there, John reached across the table and took my hand. "Don't put me off any longer, Ann," he said. "I really need you, now more than ever. Robert and my mother don't get along very well, and as soon as I can gracefully get her to leave, we will get married, and Robert and your boys will all become *our* family." As he was talking, he glanced at a couple at the next table, who greeted him.

"Maybe you were right," he continued. "This is awkward. The people at the next table are a doctor friend and his wife. She was an acquaintance of Joan's and I feel certain they'll stop to offer their condolences. I'll just say you are my sister Julia."

"They'll never believe it if you keep on holding my hand," I smiled as I took my hand from his.

Sure enough, in a minute the couple from the next table came over, and John introduced me as his sister Julia, visiting from the valley. I was afraid they would spend a while talking with us, but luckily the place was crowded and they left.

Several weeks later, his sister Julia did indeed come to town, and John insisted we all go out to dinner together. Was I ever surprised to see Julia! The resemblance was definitely there. We were exactly the same size, had the same coloring, and could have passed for sisters (she being the quieter one). We had a delightful evening, and Julia told her brother he should think about marrying "someone like Ann." Certainly it would be the best solution for Robert, who was becoming an unruly handful for Mrs. Hill.

In May John and I attended an evening gathering at one of the large hotels. As we got in the elevator to leave, a man spoke to John, saying how glad he was to see him, and that he'd see him the following Tuesday.

"I couldn't live without him," John said. "He has his own pharmaceutical company and manufactures amphetamines." I knew John took a lot of pills, but I never realized they were so necessary to him, or even what they were. I had supposed they were vitamins.

The first time John took me to see his music room, he made quite a production out of it. He took me up the winding stairs and had me wait in the hall while he went to put our favorite Rachmaninoff Concerto on the phonograph. He opened the double doors onto an anteroom and ushered me in ceremoniously. It was a beautiful intimate setting with gold carpet, white walls with ornate molding, a lovely chandelier, and an area where guests could be served refreshments.

Then he opened another set of huge double doors to a magnificent ballroom of massive proportions. The ceiling was two stories high, and the room stretched eighty feet in length and forty feet in width. There were beautiful matching chandeliers, an ornately carved marble fireplace, and magnificent pianos at either end of the room. We were engulfed by the music he had selected; it filled the entire room.

As we sat together in his Shangri-La he told me that everything in the world he wanted was in that room. He was far more relaxed than I had ever seen him and seemed totally at peace with the world. After a while he went to one of the two pianos and played his usual repertoire of favorites.

Until I saw him in these surroundings, I had never realized that he had created such a world of splendor for himself, a world that embodied all the dreams of a lifetime. When he was there, behind the closed double doors, he led the life he had envisioned for himself: cultivated, elegant, and perfect.

Because my boys were much closer to John than his own son Robert was, I feared that when he got us all together we would have some awkward moments. However, when the time rolled around and John brought Robert over, the boy was so hungry for a warm happy situation that it all worked out beautifully.

On spring weekends we went to the bay and soaked in the sun. We took the boys to a cove where we went crabbing and walked barefoot in the sand. We walked in the woods and gathered wild blackberries. The children were happy, and so were John and I. We were in love with life and with the world we had made together.

As John and Robert were leaving after one particularly delightful afternoon, John came back in and took me aside. "I can't wait any longer, baby. Let's get married this weekend. I need you, Robert needs you, and there's no reason to wait."

On June 6, John and I took all the boys to Six Flags Over Texas, and told them that we had been married privately that afternoon. They were delighted.

Those were happy days. And I believed it would last forever. Actually we were to have less than a month. John had told me that a grand jury was investigating Joan's death and that Ash Robinson was hell-bent on getting John indicted for murder! The first dark cloud had appeared on our horizon.

We all lived at my house but went to John's on occasion. I truly liked my house better, but John loved his music room, and his house was closer to the medical center. He was having a pool installed, so the yard was impossible for the boys to play in. One evening when we went by to inspect the progress on the pool, John suggested that we all spend the night there so the boys could become accustomed to their new home.

Later that evening, I went into the bathroom to brush my teeth. Without thinking, I got some toothpaste out of a top drawer and it was only when I was brushing that it dawned on me: "Ugh! John, was this Joan's drawer—is that her toothpaste? My God! Will I get hepatitis or whatever she had?" I was in tears.

He roared with laughter. "Of course not," he said.

I rushed to rinse my mouth out. "It's contagious, and if she had those germs then I'll probably get it from using her toothpaste!"

More laughing from John as he insisted that I wouldn't.

I asked if I needed to take gamma globulin or whatever?

"No, baby, really, don't worry."

But I did worry. Finally, to quiet me, he said he had

had the house fumigated and everything disinfected. (I later found out he had not.)

One evening John said he wanted to go to the medical library to research sodium pentothal, as he had sent a letter to the district attorney requesting that he be given that test to lift the cloud of suspicion from him. He took me with him and placed me in a quiet corner, while he dictated a tape on "the early concept of the lie detection test." He took notes from several books regarding the chemical content of the test; he said he wanted to find out just what he was getting himself into.

Before he was scheduled to take the test, I happened on him when he thought I was at the airport meeting his mother. However, she had missed a plane, so I arrived home unexpectedly. It was nearly time for John to be at the hospital to take the sodium pentothal test. Instead, he was in the bathroom in his shorts, with a rubber tube around his leg. I was surprised to find him there, and he was a bit shocked to see me. He explained that he had felt like he was "getting a bug, and wanted to take a shot of medication to knock it out." He complained that he couldn't find a vein.

I was upset and said I thought he should postpone the test. I knew that if a woman who was having a baby had a cold, she couldn't have an anesthetic, and that he shouldn't be taking an anesthetic if he had a "bug" either. "Please, put it off."

"No, baby, I'll be all right, leave it to me. Here, just give this to me in the seat."

"No, I can't."

"Sure, just like you give Glenn insulin, only straight in."

I was in tears then, begging him not to go. I would call and explain. He insisted; he placed the syringe and said, "Come on, baby, I'll be okay."

The syringe was cold, and larger than any I was accustomed to. After most of the solution was injected, he said, "Great, thanks, baby. That should be enough, I feel better already." And he went off all smiles, again reassuring me that he was fine.

I worried frantically about him. When he came in and went upstairs, I urged him to go right to bed. "No, baby, let me tell you about it. First, I said . . . then they said . . . then they asked me . . ." He quoted the test verbatim.

"I thought you were supposed to be *asleep* when you were asked those questions!" I said. "How is your cold? Are you all right?"

He fell on the bed laughing. "Baby, I didn't have a bug. That shot was to keep me from going to sleep." I was surprised, but relieved that he was all right. I was confused as well. John was obviously so relieved to have the test behind him. However, his mother had just come in from the airport, and dinner was ready, so we didn't talk about it again.

The days that followed were hectic but happy. John and the boys were working on their motorbikes in my garage one evening. The temptation was too much for John. He decided it looked like such fun that he got on Mel's motorbike; Jim was on his, and the two of them drove off with John looking like a little boy on his first bicycle. In a few minutes Jim came back yelling. "Quick, Mel, get on back, John is hurt," and they sped out the driveway. I got in my car and followed them to the school yard where they had been riding on the trails.

Jim ran up to me. "Mom, I think John must have broken his arm or something, we'd better get him to the hospital." He ran back to help Mel with John, and I followed him. John looked terrible. His right arm was dangling in front of him, completely out of place, and he appeared to be in shock. The entire neighborhood was there by then, and we all felt so helpless. We needed a doctor desperately, and *our* doctor was completely unable to help us. Finally his eyelids fluttered open, and he started telling us what to do. He raised himself, felt around with his left hand, and said he must have broken his collarbone. "Don't worry, baby, that's simple to fix," and with that, he slumped back to the ground.

Someone arrived with a cold towel, and a group of the boys' friends finally succeeded in carrying John to the car. We sped to the hospital; John had had one of the boys call an orthopedic surgeon to meet us there. He informed us that John would have to undergo surgery so a pin could be placed in his collarbone, but John was firm in his objection. "That will be impossible. That would mean surgery twice. Once to place the pin, another time to remove it. There's just no way I'm going to go through that."

John was in terrible pain, and the doctor was flustered over his refusal. "But, John, it's the best way to mend in this case. Look at the X-rays yourself." And he turned pleadingly to me. "I'm sure you agree, Mrs. Hill, we want this thing handled properly."

John turned quietly to me. "Baby, I just can't go through all that." His face was pale and his shoulder looked pathetically caved in. He turned to the doctor. "Just get me a figure eight bandage, and some xylocaine block. I'm sure it will mend all right; I have a busy surgical schedule for the next several weeks myself." The orthopedist gave in and consented to let the physician attempt to heal himself.

As we drove home, John tried to mask his discomfort, but I could tell he was still in considerable pain. When we were alone, I asked him why he wouldn't get the pin in his shoulder. "Surgery is for *other people,* baby, not me. The same goes for motorbikes!" He tried to laugh it off. It didn't occur to me until much later that John was concerned over the anesthetic more than anything else.

He spent a restless night, and early the next morning, I found him in the bathroom giving himself another xylocaine block to deaden the pain. After a cup of coffee he declared himself fit enough to drive off to the hospital and perform surgery. There was no talking him out of it, and he did look a little better, even though he was black-and-blue and tightly bound across the shoulders.

John took massive doses of another pain killer, as well as the xylocaine, during the next couple of days; he told me he had had to drop out and take more xylocaine several times in the middle of an operation when the pain became unbearable. He was concerned that the nurses and assistants might have noticed, and of course, they did. He even had to find a site in his back for the injections because he had used all the places he could reach in front. Finally, he began to feel better, but it had been a terrible ordeal for him.

In late June, 1969, John and I were having dinner at a restaurant when suddenly he blurted out, "I wish all those people would quit looking at me—quit giving me the 'fish eye.' " I assured him they were probably admiring him—or his wife (just being silly).

"I mean it," he said. "Every time I'm paged at a hospital and they say 'Dr. John Hill,' I can feel all eyes turning to stare at me. I thought when I took the sodium pentothal test that would, put an end to any suspicion once and for all."

"Well," I said, "I just wish you'd taken it under the proper circumstances."

"Don't say that!" John jumped up and leaned across the table. "Why did you say that? Don't ever mention that again!" (He was talking quite loud, and indeed people *did* stare then!)

I just looked at him in disbelief. He had never been anything but perfectly polite to me. I had never heard him raise his voice. John looked around and realized he was causing a scene.

"Darling, I'm sorry I got so upset." He sat down. "Waitress, bring her another drink." He turned back to me. "Darling, I just never thought you would bring that up."

"John, *I* didn't bring it up. *You* brought the subject up. I have never said anything about it. Of course, I didn't think you'd exactly get a Heisman trophy for the way you handled it. But I never have said anything about it." (Now, of course, I realize that with that statement I was saying quite a mouthful, and John must have suddenly realized I hadn't overlooked the incident, but there was not another mention of it.)

He came around and sat beside me in the booth. "Darling, I'm so sorry," he said with much affection. "I love you so. I've just been on edge. Please forgive me."

After dinner we went to Herman Hospital. John excused himself for a minute. I assumed he had some medical records to dictate, as I knew he had no patients there. Every day John had a card typed for each of us, listing his schedule for the day, usually surgery every morning and patients at one of his two offices in the afternoon. The names of patients in various hospitals where he would be making his evening rounds were also listed.

After about forty-five minutes, I went to the telephone and asked the hospital operator where Dr. Hill was. She said he had answered a page from surgery a while ago. I went to the doctors' lounge outside surgery, and when an orderly came out and said good evening, I asked him if Dr. Hill was in the operating room.

"Yes, m'am, Dr. John Hill sure is in there, but there's no surgery. He's probably coming right out."

Shortly after, John came out, behaving very matter of factly and giving no explanation. He had had a lot of trouble securing enough xylocaine to remain free of pain, and I assumed he had gone to the hospital to get some. When we got in the car, he started driving in a direction that would not lead to either of our homes. After a while I asked where we were going.

"Just driving."

"John, let's go home. We're both exhausted. There's no baby sitter with the children and you have surgery in about five hours."

He didn't answer, and I noticed a peculiar look on his face. There was an unusual silence while he fiddled with the radio. Then he stopped and adjusted his seat belt—I never fasten one.

Finally, at about two or so in the morning, we were out in the country and I said I needed to go to the bathroom. When John turned the car around and started back, I put my head in his lap. Suddenly he pulled over and stopped, and I popped up. "What are you doing?"

My only answer was a blank look from John. I asked if his collarbone was hurting; I rubbed his neck and said I'd drive.

"No, I'll drive." He started racing the car, driving wildly.

"For God's sake, John, I *am* in a hurry to get home, but I want to get there all in one piece." In the reflection of the dash lights I saw a very peculiar look on his face. Really diabolical. His voice was cruel and strange, yet it sounded as if he were proud of what he was saying.

"I didn't want it to have to be this way. I thought Joan would see I could never live with her. I loved you so much, but I knew you'd never wait till a divorce could go through. Then when Ash wrote out that agreement for me to sign, and Joan was laughing all over town about it, I knew, right then, that her own father had just authored her death certificate. After all—there comes a time when some people are no longer meant for this world. I couldn't let what we had go—

"But it was all really so easy," he continued. "First I got some Petri dishes from the lab, and then I grew some cultures." (I remembered the "experiment.") "I saved every form of human excretion. Urine, feces, pus from a boil on a patient's back."

My flesh was *crawling,* but I listened, hypnotized by this strange dialogue from a person who only cruelly, grotesquely resembled my beloved John. Everything he said had the ring of truth. I never said a word. As he went on talking, I thought, "I'll never let you touch me again." (Little did I know that that was not going to be my problem!)

His face was a mask of evil; his eyes piercingly cruel and his features contorted. His voice had taken on a diabolical tone. "First, I gave it to her in some pastries. Nothing happened. Then I gave her some ipecac in a Coke. She threw up everything but her toenails. Then she begged me to do something for her. She was sweet about it, really. So I gave her a broad-spectrum anti-biotic, Mysteclin mixed in with the result of the cultures, and from then on, it was just a matter of time. By the time I took her to the hospital she was in irreversible shock."

I was *ill.* Dumbfounded. He actually sounded *proud.* My heart was pounding wildly and my voice, choked with fear, was lost somewhere deep within me. How could this transformation have taken place? Who was this frightening monster? Where was John?

But it *was* John—this cold, calculating demon whose very person was somehow commingled with that of my husband. I was terrified. Too frightened to think. Too horrified to move.

The car turned off onto a road, dirt or gravel—I couldn't be sure which from the sound. There were white fences on my right.

"Where are we, John?"

He turned the car around, and looked toward the fences. In a horrible, chilling voice he said, "That's where someone used to live—who doesn't live any-more." (It was Joan's horse farm.)

He drew up at a stop sign, then turned fast to the right, going forty or fifty miles an hour, and, in about the next fifty feet, suddenly said:

"AND, NOW, NEITHER ARE YOU!"

"John, John—don't"— I struggled to get the wheel.
No luck. I slid all the way over on his side of the car.
There was an awful slam as the car rammed into the
concrete bridge.

The glass of the windshield shattered. And kept shat-
tering . . .

The *horror* of what he had said.

The *nightmare* he had described.

The unreality of it all.

He looked at me—I was very much alive, although
the right front wheel was all but in my face and my
side of the car was totaled like an accordion.

"John, my God, John, why did you do that? I smell
gasoline, we're going to catch on fire! Let's get out!"
His nose was gushing blood. "John—are you all right,
John?"

No—he certainly wasn't all right. He looked at me
with that indescribable expression that had changed his
face—his very being. I was consumed with fear. Out
of his pocket, he pulled a syringe! Never saying a word,
he struggled to get it aimed at me. I was way over next
to him on his side of the seat—I had no place to
move to.

"My God, John—don't do that! For God's sake!—I
smell gasoline—let's get out, *please!*"

"You'll never get out," he told me with a terrible
smile.

I managed to throw him off balance, and the syringe
fell to the floor in the wreckage on my side.

"Come on, John." Like a flash, out came another
syringe! I was drained of all energy.

I put my arms around his neck and looked at him.
His body was foreign to my touch. His face was gro-
tesque and his eyes held an atrociously wicked look.
With all the resolve I possessed, I quietly pleaded:
"Please, John, don't do this. I love you, John. Let's

just get out of here. I swear to God I'll never mention this again."

We both became aware of car lights approaching us from the rear, reflecting on our car.

"Throw that away—get out quick, John, before we catch on fire."

John threw the syringe over the bridge. (It has since been recovered. After exhaustive tests the contents were shown to be procaine hydrochloride which would have made my heart fibrillate, causing death in seconds, according to the pathologist. I would have appeared to have died of shock following the wreck.)

People from the other car approached us and asked if we were all right. John was pleasant, though nervous, and assured them we were not seriously injured, then asked: "Would you please take us to Sharpstown Hospital? My wife seems rather hysterical."

"No," I sobbed, "not to Sharpstown." (Joan had died there.)

"Let's make it Memorial Baptist, please"—where John *never* practiced.

I was sobbing. "But, John . . ."

It was dark and I was terrified with this strange version of John beside me, holding me close, whispering: "Don't say a word, baby." (What a relief, it was in the loving familiar voice.) I turned and my eyes searched in the dark for the well-loved face. In the dim light his features blurred beside me; he seemed to feel me looking at him.

"Ann." I looked away. The sound of his voice saying my name so tenderly brought tears streaming silently down my cheeks. Everything he had said ran through my mind over and over. I couldn't stop doing an instant replay on the events he had described. It couldn't be so. It mustn't be so.

But it all had such a ring of authenticity. The ipecac, the "experiment" in his apartment. Everything swirled around in my mind. How *could* he? What had caused the change in him that brought on the maniacal events he had described to me? Could he really have taken Joan's life in the fiendish way he had so vividly described? My whole world was falling apart before me. I was dizzy and faint.

We pulled up to Memorial Baptist Hospital. John thanked the people who had given us a ride and assured them that we would be fine. He asked if they could please go back and wait for the police and a wrecker; he said he would call to report the accident right away.

He took me into the emergency room and assured the nurse on duty that he was Dr. John Hill, showed her some identification and told her he could handle our injuries, so she left us alone. John stopped his nosebleed and then turned his attention to my cuts and bruises. He put some stitches in my knee and reassured me that there was nothing seriously wrong.

At first I couldn't bring myself to look at him closely, fearing I would again see that chilling look on his face. I was sitting on the examining table and he was working on my knee. I studied my husband, as his hands expertly performed their accustomed tasks of repair. He was concerned and anxious-looking. Finally, I reached out, with tears in my eyes, and touched his head. "John?" I said.

His eyes would not meet mine. "Just a minute, baby." He noticed I was very nervous. My hand was trembling, and he kissed it. John wanted to give me some medication to calm me down, but was not insistent when I tearfully declined the offer. He still would not look me in the eye.

I asked John what was in the syringes he had tried to inject me with. "It was just distilled water," he said. "I just wanted to scare you so you wouldn't bring up the sodium pentothal test or Joan's death, or anything else about it, ever again. Let's don't talk about it, baby."

I cringed in pain as he removed a splinter of glass

from my leg. I tried to fix my mind on something else —but the recent events came back again. Who was the monster who had sat there gloating as he described what had happened to Joan? Could the John I knew *really* do those things?

And what about me? *Why, why* had he turned on me? Was he so upset over my comment regarding the lie detector test? Was he so cold and calculating he could then see only one solution to my telling anyone, or even mentioning it to him? What could I do?

I wanted to ask him, but I couldn't bear to put it in words. I wanted to find a way to make it all not so. I was in a state of shock. John knew how I felt, and he tried to comfort me.

I asked John what he thought people would say if his second wife died within three months of his first wife. "I guess I just didn't think it through. I'm sorry, baby. Please let's don't talk about it ever again. Remember, you promised." I realized then that if I were not careful I would not *live* to leave him, and that I had better drop the subject.

As he cleaned up, I continued to watch his every move, afraid to rclax. I studied his reflection in the mirror as he scrubbed his hands. He looked up, and our eyes met. I couldn't help it—tears ran down my cheeks; he turned and came to me. "Ann, please, baby. Please!"

I pulled back when he put his arms around me.

"Don't. Don't ever pull away from me. I know I acted in a despicable way." He looked at me directly then. "I beg you to forgive me. I'll make you forget this ever happened." His chin quivered. "I know it was unforgivable, but I swear I'll make it up to you." We were interrupted by a nurse who came to the door to see if we were finished. John had phoned the police to report the accident and had then called a taxi to take us home. Once we were in the cab, he decided that we should go back and check on the car to make certain that a wrecker came and towed it away.

When I saw the wreck, I was upset all over again. The police were there; they asked if there were any passengers and, when they saw my side of the car, they couldn't believe I had survived. John insisted on doing all the talking. "Baby, go get that syringe on the floor in front and put it in your purse." Meanwhile he was busy getting some things out of the trunk. An officer came around by the driver's seat where I was searching with a flashlight, and asked, "Can I help you, Mrs. Hill?" I had just slipped the syringe in my purse. "No thanks," I told him. "I was just seeing if anything dropped out of my purse," and as I got out again, John rushed up to see what we were talking about.

The policeman turned his flashlight on me; he noticed my bloody dress and looked at me closely. "Lady, are you absolutely sure you are all right?" My eyes were red from crying and I'm sure I didn't look too collected.

John spoke up immediately. "Of course. She's upset, but I've taken care of her injuries, thank you. She's fine, aren't you, baby?" Then, with a squeeze and a reassuring smile, he said, "We really must be going, officer, thank you so very much."

Not so easily dismissed, the officer said, "How did this happen, doctor?"

"Well," John stammered, "I have a broken collarbone from a motorcycle accident and I must have had a muscle spasm." He had told the people who picked us up that he had dozed off at the wheel. He was going to have to get his stories straight. And he was going to have to get a lot more straight with me.

My fright was not so easily forgotten. I wasn't in the mood for an argument or a discussion at that point; I was so thankful to be alive. For the time being, I would drop the subject. If I could convince him not to take my life, as I had when the car approached, maybe

I could find the means to discover the answers to all the questions that swam through my mind.

We got back in the taxi, and John put his medical bag and some boxes from his car in beside us. He told the driver to take us to his address on Kirby Drive.

"No, John, the children are at my house."

"Yes, baby, but I need to leave these things at my place; we can get Joan's car out of the garage." I had forgotten her car had been there all that time. John had planned to get rid of it but never had gotten around to it.

When the taxi pulled up in front of his house, John got out and unlocked the front door, then came back to get me. "Come on, baby, let's go up and get a little nap, shall we? I have to be in surgery in less than two hours."

"No, John, I'll just wait on the front porch. We have to go to my house so I can get the boys started for the day."

He looked at me with both hurt and understanding in his eyes. "All right, honey, I'll get the car. Don't be afraid of me, Ann. Please, I can't explain it myself, so I don't know how I can make you understand. But I'll show you nothing is wrong. I love you, baby. Please, please, forgive me." He moved to put his arms around me, and I pulled back.

While John put his things in the front hall, I reached in my purse quickly, took out the syringe and hid it in the grass bordering the front steps. John went to get the car, calling out, "I'll just be a minute." When he pulled around in front, I got in; John reached over and held my hand, and we drove to my house in silence.

I felt much better in my own territory. When we went to bed at my house, I couldn't get to sleep. John put his arms around me, but I just sobbed and sobbed.

"I'm so sorry. I know I shouldn't have behaved that way," he explained.

"But why did you kill Joan? I thought she had

agreed to go through with a divorce. How could you *do* that?"

"I can't explain it, Ann, except to say I felt compelled to take the matter into my own hands. She wouldn't give me a divorce, and Ash was determined to ruin me if I left her again. It was the only thing I could do. After all, she had had a good life. She was through with me, anyway. And I was more than finished with her. There was no reason to continue. And I've always felt that there comes a time when some people are no longer meant for this world. I should never have turned against you. It's incomprehensible to me, too. I love you, baby. I'll make it all up to you. You'll forget all about it. Just tell yourself this night never happened."

In the early hours the alarm went off, and John bounced up, ready for surgery. Before he left, he said, "I'll take that syringe to Shilstone Testing Lab; they can tell you it only had distilled water in it." He seemed relieved when I told him I had thrown it away.

Once I found myself alone, my first instinct was to get in my car and go far, far away, but the boys had company and I couldn't just leave them. The reality of my daily routine, as well as being sore from the wreck and having a splitting headache from the long night before, kept me from fleeing John's reach. He called before beginning surgery and made plans to meet for lunch. He spoke in the same tone of voice I was accustomed to, and it was the most reassuring sound in the world. In the light of day I could hardly believe the events of the night before. Before noon flowers and a loving note arrived from John. When we met for lunch, I tried to be as cheerful and normal as possible. During lunch John showered me with attention and concern.

Activities with the children coupled with numbness caused by fright kept me close to home where I felt safe. To run away to some strange place would only add to my insecurity. I was immobilized by fear.

I fantasized about how I might get away from John. If I went to my parents, he would know. What would I do about the boys? The four of us would be easy to find any place in the world. I knew John would stop at nothing to find me. And what about Robert? I was his mother now, and he couldn't be abandoned, left to a father who might turn violently against him. I plotted as carefully and as fruitlessly as any prisoner dreaming of freedom. I would be carefully watchful. I would bide my time. I knew if I botched it, I wouldn't live to try again. I would find a way to remain safe and alive until I could get us all away.

A few days later, in July, John asked me to meet him at his house and bring my Thunderbird. He was trading in my car for a Cadillac.

"John, that's awfully sweet, but I love my car. I ordered the color specially, and I haven't had it but a year."

"No, I've already got the dealership delivering an El Dorado, and I think I'll get a Mark III brought over too. If you like it better, I'll get you a Continental. I don't know what to do with Joan's car. Mine is completely totaled, so I need to make some decision. Maybe I'll get a station wagon. Then we'll be all set when we go pick up Mel after camp." John knew I had always liked the idea of future plans. They gave me a feeling of reassurance, and I'm sure John sensed I needed this. A few days later the local paper ran an item in the gossip column to the effect that "Dr. John Hill gifted his bride with a new El Dorado."

Shortly thereafter I went to his house to look for the syringe I had hidden; it was *gone!* The yardman had been there and must have raked it up. Or else John had seen me put it there and had gotten it himself.

In the days that followed, John did everything he could to make me forget. At one point I told him I wanted some time alone, to realign my thoughts and try to regain my balance. "I'm not at all sure I can go on after all this, John," I told him.

"Don't ever say that, baby! Don't *ever* talk like that. Don't even think that way. I'll never let you get away. If you ever left me, I would kill myself. There would be no reason to go on. I won't let you feel this way. You upset me—to think that these thoughts would ever enter your mind."

He assured me that if I tried to leave him, he would get to me, wherever in the world I went. So the best thing to do was to forget. Yet every time I was out of his sight, he quizzed me about who I had seen or talked to.

But who could I talk to? I was alone on an island of our own design with John. We had never *wanted* other people around. Our world consisted of our children and my parents, and the least intrusion possible from the outside.

John knew this as well as I. But my panic, like that of a wounded trapped bird, left him wondering what I might do if I could fly. I felt as if I were beating myself to death in a cage. I was petrified, immobilized with fright. There had to be some kind of solution that wouldn't leave me feeling so numb.

Mel was due to leave for camp in a few days. We were at my house packing his things when he noticed I was crying.

"Mom, what is it?"

"Oh, Mel, I can't talk about it. I'm just upset, and there is nothing anyone can do but let some time go by, I guess."

"You're probably still shook up after the wreck the other night," he suggested.

"Yes, yes, that's it, Mel. I guess when you come close to death it makes you think about the possibility of something happening, and you boys not having me anymore. I want you to promise me something—"

I stammered—how could I put it?

"Just be certain," I said, "if I should ever die, be positive what caused it. Insist on an autopsy."

"Oh, Mom, nothing is going to happen to you. I didn't think the wreck with John was so bad. You're more upset than I realized. You're just trying to do too much."

"Mel, you're going away tomorrow. It's a year since we were all at camp, when we met John. Do you remember?"

"How could I forget?" he laughed. "Remember the canoe?" He was trying to get me to laugh.

"Yes, but Mel, so much has happened—I'll be all right, but let me say this to you, please. In case anything should ever happen to me—"

"Would we live with Dad?"

"Yes, you would live with Melvin. Just please promise me you'll check it out. Papa would help you. Remember, like we checked with the FAA after Aunt Jean and Uncle Drew's plane crash? Find out what caused it, promise me."

"Mom, what are you trying to say?"

"I'm trying to say I'm upset. You're leaving tomorrow. I'll be alone with just your brothers. You've looked out for us all for so long. And—"

"But John will be here."

"I know. And you'll be back soon. John already has our reservations to pick you up in August. Forgive me for being so weepy."

There are some things that there is just no way to discuss with someone else, I guess. I had to find some peace of mind. I tried to find it with John. When he touched me, I cringed (to our mutual dismay). When I was alone, I was haunted by his words, and the picture of his description of how he caused Joan's death wouldn't leave my mind. I knew it just wasn't one of those things that, given time, would diminish and fade. It's hard to say what bothered me most. The ghastly end that Joan had come to—Was it because of me?

Should I have known? Was there some way I could have prevented it? Could I change it now? Could I help John discover that perhaps Joan had had a heart attack or died as the result of some other natural cause? Could I *ever* put this out of my mind? How could he do it? How could I ever ever love him again?

If what he said was true, how could I not have seen it coming or had *some* hint of all the horror that was to come? How could he be all the things I thought he was —and this terrible *monster* as well? Mr. Hyde, indeed! Could he really be capable of being so wonderful and loving to me and my children, then change to a grotesque and diabolical genius concocting death for others as a remedy to his problems?

How could I *cope?* Or *think?* Or *eat?* Or *sleep?* Were none of life's normal functions ever to be mine again?

Where was the John I had known and loved? I felt sick, deep in the pit of my stomach. The very person I had loved so deeply, the one who had rekindled the flame long dead within me, was not the wonderful person I thought he was. I was haunted by the feeling of betrayal. How could I have misjudged him so?

Yet I could think of nothing that would have forewarned me. Certainly we had known each other well enough. But perhaps none of us can truly know the depths beneath the surface of another person. Ash Robinson was one of the few who sensed the dark side that John kept hidden from the rest of the world.

At times John would walk into the room, familiar and loving, and I would find myself filled with relief. What had I been so upset about? Then, like a flash— never with any warning—it would come back. And our island in life would be flooded with all the torment of what he had told me. I was once again back at the bridge—my world crashing to pieces all around me.

But not quite to pieces. After all, I had been able to talk John out of hurting me (what an understatement).

Maybe it was something that was over and done—never to be repeated again. Maybe if I could find a way to cut it out of my mind . . .

I tried to be myself. Who was I, really? Was I so important to John that I had caused him to take the life of his wife to avoid the risk of losing what we had together? Didn't that make me some kind of a monster, too? Yet I hadn't felt like a monster. I would give anything to be back the way we were, before all this had happened. If he had only discussed it with me, certainly we could have come to a better solution and Joan would still be alive.

For my sanity, for my children, for John, and what good influence I could ever be on him, I *had* to find a way to handle this. A way to be all the good things I knew we could be and had been together. After all, in large part, any chance of recouping our best selves was up to me.

I told myself I would try to ignore it. But I couldn't. I would try to find a way to ascertain that it had happened another way. I *had* to.

"Life goes on," John said. (Promise?—Mine too?) "Make the best of it, baby. We've got each other. It's what we both wanted. I hadn't intended . . ." Oh no, don't say it all again!!!

Time would help. I knew it. It *had* to.

I would try John's method. He frequently wrote me notes, so I wrote one to him:

My dearest John,

Please know how very sorry I am to find myself so sensitive, and so crushed with disappointment.

I want so much to NOT be hurt.

I have tried to think of all the ways NOT to let it matter.

Let me find a way, with your help, to understand, or to at least accept the situation.

We have, each of us, too much to give to the

other ever to think of throwing it away. What a crime that would be—to deliberately turn off such a lot of love.

I need to know that I can believe in you, and that my feelings are first and foremost in your life.

Try, if you can, to see this from my point of view. Then maybe together we can arrive at a solution to my distress.

I want to be all the things to you that make us the best of what we are—together.

Ann

I found I couldn't drop the subject with John. He tried to frighten me into silence. One day he asked me to drop by his house and get some papers out of the front hall. When I went in, the phone was ringing. It was John. "Baby, please go upstairs and look for my old briefcase. It should be in the closet upstairs, behind the walk-in closet in the dressing room."

"John—someone has been here. All the papers you had in the front hall are messed up."

"There couldn't have been, honey. You and I are the only ones who have keys, and I was only outside checking on the pool this morning. Try to find my briefcase, and I'll come get you for lunch."

I went to check on the pool and turned the water off, then went in to see about the briefcase John needed. I stopped again in the entry. I *knew* it hadn't looked like that when we were there last.

I went upstairs to John's dressing room, and into what had been Joan's closet. The week before, all her things had been moved to her parents' house. It was dark and I was in a hurry.

I opened the doors, and my God! there, staring at me, was Joan! Only after an awful moment did I realize that it was a wig stand, with Joan's face drawn on it. Joan's fall was styled as I wore my hair (not in the ponytail she always wore). Her clothes had been arranged to look as though she were standing there in real life!

I ran down the stairs, absolutely terrified, just as John walked in the front door.

"What's the matter, baby?"

I pushed past him and got in my car. I was sobbing hysterically. He never said a word, never went in to see what had scared me. Why should he? He knew. A plastic surgeon could easily reproduce Joan's face. And that face looked exactly like Joan.

John drove me to lunch and tried to talk about other things to distract me. He almost succeeded. As he was talking, once again he was the person I loved, that sweet face, that loving voice; then, without warning, tears started running down my cheeks. John reached over and held my hand, tight. He didn't have to ask what was the matter. He knew.

"What are you trying to do to me, John, scare me to death? I just can't get used to being married to a *murderer*."

It was a cruel thing to say, but I felt that way, and John understood. "I'd give anything if I hadn't told you. I should have known how it would affect you. I've learned too late I shouldn't have told you," John went on. "It was a burden I should not have called on you to share. We should all keep some things to our innermost selves. There are things I have done that seemed to me the proper solution at the time. I did what I felt would be for the best and was content in that knowledge. Those things, like a story taken out of context, are out of place when presented to others in a different light. There is no need to let it make a difference. I can accept it. There were situations that I tolerated up to a point, then handled in the manner I chose to. But I should never have burdened my 'baby' with these things. Don't be perturbed, I'll find a way to make it all right for us both."

He asked me to please drop by the Cadillac place, where his wrecked car was, and check it out for anything of his, whatever might be in the trunk or car, and please bring it to him at the office. He had patients waiting, and would be there all afternoon.

The people at the car dealer's directed me to the wrecked car. I walked into the dimly lit building, and as I saw the crumbled wreckage, it hit me all over again. "Can we help you, lady?" a couple of workmen asked.

I said I had just come to get some things out of the car. They saw how upset I was, and offered to help. "Lady, that sure was a bad accident. Did you lose a loved one in it?"

I shook my head. "No, *I* am the 'loved one.' "

John's surgical equipment was strewn all over the wreckage. When I took John his belongings I told him what the men had said. And once again I dissolved into tears. I was really in bad shape. He knew I wouldn't take anything he gave me. He opened a drawer filled with medical samples and said, "Take anything you want. Those are tranquilizers, those others will make you sleep." I told him I needed a "mood elevator," one guaranteed to go "up," not "down." He showed me where they were, and I took one. While John went back to his patients, I sat in his office, sipping a Coke and trying to calm down.

Hedy, one of his nurses, came in and saw the state I was in. "He's got you upset, hasn't he, hon? Well, he used to upset Joan, too. I just don't know what it is about him that makes him do the things he does. You should have seen the way he broke down and told me all sorts of things when I took him to select her grave site. He just went completely to pieces and told me everything! I mean everything! I know things about him that would make your hair stand on end!"

I was amazed at the chummy tone John's nurse was taking, but not at all interested in gossiping with her about my husband. Later I mentioned to John that Hedy was really talking about him, and I wondered why he kept her on.

"I couldn't manage the office without her," he replied. "She runs everything and covers for me when I'm late for appointments. She would do anything in the world for me. I'm sure she would never discuss anything I didn't want talked about. What did she say? Did she tell you anything about that malpractice suit?"

"What malpractice suit?" I asked.

"We've been having a time with a former patient who has instigated a huge lawsuit, claiming I botched a breast reduction procedure. That's the reason I always take before-and-after photographs. She was in much worse shape before I performed the surgery; now she's claiming she wants $250,000 because she didn't turn out perfectly. Hedy's been on the phone all day trying to get some malpractice insurance for me. Mine was canceled, and I don't know what to do. Lloyds of London may not even take me now. Hedy shouldn't have mentioned it to you."

Hedy *hadn't* mentioned it. My knowledge of my husband was increasing at a faster rate, and with worse revelations than I could assimilate or cope with.

John could see I was in such bad shape that there was no telling what I would do. He kept asking if I had seen or talked to my father. I'm sure he knew that if I saw him I would disintegrate and tell him the whole story. He tried to keep me busy and reassured that all was well. He knew I was scared to death of him.

We were invited to a birthday party at my cousin Mary's. The entire family was there, and I hoped to get my mind on other things and enjoy the evening. But I was so shaky I dropped a pitcher of punch. Mary took me into her bedroom and quizzed me.

"Ann, what's *wrong* with you? I've never seen you like this. Have you and John had a fight? I notice you are avoiding him. In fact, you act as though you have developed an allergy to him. I know your parents have noticed too. You really ought to try to fake it, or cover up your feelings around them. Whatever it is will work out. I've never seen anyone so crazy about another person as John is about you. So whatever is wrong between you, it can't be all that bad."

"Oh, Mary, it's just that awful wreck we were in. I've been upset ever since. I know I'm not at my best, but I'll shape up. Really, I will."

John was quick to ask Mary what we had been talking about. She reassured him when she said, "I was just giving your bride a little pep talk. You ought to give her some vitamins, she's not her usual 'spunky self.' "

I finally devised a "life insurance" plan for myself. I told John I had written down every word he had said and had placed the document in a safe deposit box, to which my father had the key. So, if anything ever happened to me, everything would be known. This had a very sobering effect on John.

So, for a time, we had a sort of moratorium. We were going to make it work. After all, it was pointless not to. The damage had been done. I *had* to disregard the questions I didn't like his answers to. I *had* to get to be me again. John was still himself, if I would just let him be, if I would just quit bugging him. He never wanted to bring up the subject of what had happened to Joan. The trouble was, when I brought it up, the answers were always the same, and never what I wanted to hear.

We were invited to a party honoring some friends who had just been married. As we were enjoying the champagne and toasting the bride and groom, I noticed Jack Ramsay across the room. Our eyes met and held. John was watching. Jack broke away from the group he was with and came over and gave me a big hug. "Well, there you are! You sure keep her all to yourself, John! How are you?" he asked politely of John. Then he turned to me, and said in an intimate

Joan Robinson as a young equestrienne

Joan Robinson Hill in the show ring

Joan among her trophies

Joan and John cutting their wedding cake

Joan with her parents and husband John Hill

Ann, when she was planning to go to New York to be a Conover model. At her parents' urging, she went home and married her high school beau instead.

John when he was named a "fellow" of the American College of Surgeons

*John's brother,
Julian Hill*

*Ann's son Jim, her father, John and Joan Hill's son Robert
(center), and cousin Mary Ann*

Dr. John Hill's home

The car in which John tried to kill Ann

Ann and John shortly before their separation

Ann Kurth today surrounded by her three sons, Jim, Glenn, and Mel

tone, "Honey, you look terrific! You don't know how I miss you."

I had been totally committed to John, and the last thing I wanted was to ever see him feel uncomfortable—certainly he had no reason to be jealous, but it *was* awkward. Jack's date didn't like it much either, and came over and lured her escort away.

John was terribly upset. This had never happened before. I made it a point to be especially demonstrative and hopefully reinforce the props that had been knocked out from under him. He mentioned the incident later that night, saying he couldn't bear seeing Jack gushing all over me. Trying to eradicate the encounter from John's mind was an all-night project. I could tell he was upset, and the intensity of his feelings concerned me.

During this period we were so caught up in our own family routine that outsiders scarcely penetrated our togetherness. I already had enough problems without letting someone else rock the boat.

John's associate, Dr. Moore, had decided to terminate their partnership, and there had been bedlam in the office. Mrs. Johnson, the long-time office manager, was fired; then John discovered she had taken all his records. In order to retrieve them, he was forced to write her a letter of recommendation. In the midst of all this, Ash Robinson was pressing for financial details in order to settle Joan's estate. John asked me to please help at the office until some order could be restored.

I was glad for any diversion from my problems, and realized John would reach the breaking point without my help. Eventually the office situation settled back to normal; then the next problem loomed on the horizon.

Sometime in August, Ash Robinson persuaded the district attorney to have Joan's body exhumed, and an autopsy performed. It was six months after her burial. The papers gave it a lot of attention. "A famous pathologist, Dr. Milton Helpern, who had solved the

Coppolino murder case, is coming from New York to perform the autopsy." Dr. Helpern was an almost legendary figure in the world of forensic medicine. He was the man who brought Dr. Carl Coppolino to trial on charges of killing two wives with an exotic and almost undetectable drug.

I went to a bookstore and got a copy of a book about the Coppolino murders and read it. Dr. Coppolino had even had one of the bodies exhumed on a rainy day after the funeral. The resulting moisture had caused the body to deteriorate even more rapidly. That case also involved children who were not allowed to visit their grandparents. I asked John if he had read the book. He said no, but for me to tell him about it. I did; his reaction: "These things aren't as uncommon as you might think."

The day for the exhumation and autopsy arrived. John was tense and nervous. There would be a team of nine doctors to determine the cause of death of Joan Robinson Hill, half selected by Mr. Robinson, and half by John Hill, plus Dr. Helpern.

What a long, horrible day. The autopsy lasted most of the day and was referred to hourly on the news. I *had* to ask John what he thought the outcome would be. He was concerned but confident. "There's nothing they *can* find. There were no foreign or toxic substances introduced into her body. I've already *told* them about the antibiotic I gave Joan, so that's what they have to go on."

After what seemed an endless wait, one of the doctors on John's team called to say that his autopsy report was ready, and that John could have a copy of the report. We were on our way out the door and John had his arm around me. "Perk up, baby—it's going to be all right—I know it is." He gave me a hug and a kiss (*he* was trying to cheer *me* up!).

As we pulled out the driveway, Mr. Robinson, who lived nearby, was walking home, dejectedly. He had been hiding in the bushes and had seen the loving scene on our porch. Poor man, I didn't blame him for being upset.

Ash had gotten into the habit of parking at the side of the house in the hopes of catching a glimpse of his grandson. Sometimes he'd come into the yard to see Robert—it was scary when he appeared in the bushes, but understandable. I asked John, when this autopsy business was finished, to please reconsider and let Robert go visit his grandparents. John was adamant that Robert was never to see them and must make haste to get inside whenever Ash appeared.

We went by to pick up the autopsy report, and proceeded, as planned, to take the boys to our favorite Mexican restaurant. The children sat at another table. We ordered and then John said, "Excuse me, baby, let me just glance over this report."

He read hastily, then flipped through to the last page, noncommittally. I inquired as to the results. "Inconclusive. But not too good. It says she died *with* a massive infection of undetermined origin. Not *of* a massive infection."

"What's the difference?"

"All the world. If she had died *of* a massive infection, then that would be the answer. This merely leaves it open. They say she died *with* a massive infection. It's like saying she died *with* a cold, or *with* an ingrown toenail, but it would not be the *cause* of death. The cause is still not determined. It leaves it open to speculation."

He seemed agitated.

"Let me see it."

"No, darling. You wouldn't understand. It's all medical technology. You wouldn't understand."

Dinner came, and John continued to pore over the autopsy report, totally engrossed.

"Sorry, baby, but you know this is important. Waiter, one more order of enchiladas, please."

He was wolfing his dinner down while reading the autopsy report. But I had learned not to question him, even though it made me queasy to see him reading about Joan's death while eating!

We left the restaurant and went home. I asked again to read the report.

"No, baby, it will upset you."

"Please, John. Remember, I said 'for better or worse.' If it's going to be *better,* I *deserve* to know. If it's going to be *worse,* I *need* to know."

"No, darling, I must insist, I know best in this matter." And he locked the autopsy report in a cabinet in his closet! He had several cabinets with combination locks and I had no idea what was in them.

I was really bewildered at his being so secretive. John tried to divert my attention, but I wouldn't budge. I wanted to see what in that autopsy report had him so on edge. Finally John gave in, but said, "Read it fast, baby, we need to leave and make rounds. Don't talk about it now. Just glance over it quickly."

I pored over the report. It was not too technical. I had hoped to find that Joan might have died by some other means. The first thing I noticed was a reference to the fact that the casket had *been removed previously!* (John hadn't wanted me to know that.)

"John, what could this mean? Look—it says the casket had been removed before!"

"Now, baby, come on, give me back the report. I don't want to discuss it."

"But John—Ash could have had the casket removed and done *anything* to have made it look suspicious. There's no telling what that could mean!"

"Baby, I really don't want to talk about it—"

"And look, John, it says she had a transfusion forty-five minutes before she died. If they gave her the wrong kind of blood, that could have caused her death, couldn't it, John?"

"Baby."

"Please, John, tell me, couldn't the wrong kind of blood transfusion have caused her death?"

"Yes. That could have caused her death. But it *didn't*. Come on, honey, we really have to leave. Let's don't even talk about it any more."

There I was, so hopeful I could find *another* cause for Joan's death, and John merely reaffirmed my worst fears. There *was* no other cause for her death. *He had killed her,* just like he said.

"Baby, I appreciate what you're trying to do. I know you don't want to accept what I told you about Joan's death, but you're just going to have to. You can read all nine autopsy reports when they come in. They'll probably have different versions of the same thing. The important thing is that they probably won't be conclusive. You are only going to prolong your misery if you continue to hold out hope that Joan died some other way than what I've told you. Accept it, baby, then forget it. It has nothing to do with my love for you. The best thing you can do is find a way to forget it, and maybe then we can be the way we were before Joan and Ash decided I could never have a divorce."

I had the explanation. Again. I tried to let it go at that. I was going to have to let go of the vain hope that I could find another cause of Joan's death. It's hard to turn loose of a quest for something that will bring you peace of mind.

When John left for surgery the next day, I asked Jim to help me open the cabinets in John's closet. I thought the cabinets just might hold some clue. There were six combination locks, and we couldn't figure the combination to any of them. In desperation we drove to a hardware store and bought a hacksaw and six locks identical to the ones in John's closet.

We went home and got busy sawing open all the locks. We looked through the contents of the cabinets and found mostly meaningless junk. There were several newspaper clippings, mostly about funerals. Some con-

cerned Julian's death, others were about Joan; there
was a brief obituary notice about John's father, and
some others I didn't know, and a clipping about Jack
Ramsay at a horse show (why had he saved that?).
There were also some clippings about a friend's funeral,
a "Dr. Andrew Gordon,"* and finally three interesting
items:

1. An envelope on which was written: *Mrs. Hill's
ring.* The envelope had the name of the funeral home
on it (and a bulge that might be a ring).

2. John's reference notes taken at the medical library
when he was researching sodium pentothal.

3. A strange book of illustrations and photographs,
with pages marked, showing actual before-and-after
cases of how plastic surgery had changed the faces and
fingerprints of several Nazi war criminals.

It was getting late, and I didn't want John to notice
his closet had been gone through and the cabinets
opened. Jim and I tidied up, threw away the sawed-off
locks, and replaced them with identical locks. I put the
papers in my desk and didn't mention them to John—or
the envelope with Joan's ring from the funeral home.

A few days later I heard John in his closet, muttering
to himself. He couldn't open one of the cabinets. He
looked in his billfold and got out all six combinations to
his secret hiding places. He was sure he had remembered them in the wrong sequence. He never could understand or figure it out, and he finally called a locksmith to come figure out the combinations and unlock
the cabinets for him. Jim and I had a hard time keeping
a straight face.

While Mel was at camp, my house was sold, and we
moved our things to John's house so the boys would be
settled when school started. John set up strict security
measures when he became aware of Ash's continuing
surveillance. He had me order thick new curtains all

* Fictitious name.

over the house. He had a Doberman pinscher that had
been Joan's trained as a guard dog. However, I never
had much faith in the dog's trainability against Ash,
since he had kept the dog at his house frequently when
Joan was alive. Sure enough, I saw Mr. Robinson get
out of his car one day and pet the dog, who licked him
affectionately.

Soon it was time to get Mel at camp (where we had
met just a year before); the other boys had been having
too much fun together to leave home and go to camp
that summer. We piled in the station wagon and had a
perfectly delightful trip. Being away from Houston really seemed to help. We spent a long rainy night talking.
For the first time since the wreck I was able to unwind
and be responsive to my husband. John and I discussed
the possibility of moving. We considered several places,
including Mexico, but felt that would be too difficult.
Then we talked about the possibility of buying another
house, close to the medical center. Maybe that would be
a good solution.

When we got home we looked at two or three places,
but John and I both realized there was nothing to com-
pare with the house he already had, unless we moved
twenty or thirty miles farther out. Besides, he had done
extensive remodeling to make the boys' quarters as comfortable as possible. He had finished the entire third
floor for Mel's territory. The pool was just about finished, and of course there was the music room. Nothing
could approach that, unless we built a house. Since my
father was an architect, John decided we would stay in
his home for the present, and consider having Papa design another home in the near future. We could at least
move from Ash Robinson's immediate vicinity.

By September John was having an increasingly difficult time breathing. He had broken his nose in the wreck
we were in, and it was not going to heal by itself. He
eventually consulted another plastic surgeon, who told
him that surgery would be required, and suggested John

not put it off any longer. The air passage was almost completely blocked. You can imagine his problem performing surgery with a surgical mask over his face while he was gasping for breath himself.

But John was terrified by the idea! I couldn't believe it. "Surgery is fine—for other people," he said. However, he was having such difficulty breathing that common sense prevailed. He finally consented to schedule himself for the nose operation. John was a terrible prospective patient. He made excuses to cancel the operation, then had to reschedule it when breathing became unbearably difficult.

He refused to be admitted to the hospital until the last minute. Then he asked me to go through the tunnel from the hospital to his office building and into his office for a can of spray to deaden the feeling in his face before they touched him. He was terrified by the anesthetic and asked the doctor to give him a local, but this was not possible. When they came to wheel John into surgery, he took one last squirt of skin deadener, and was pushed down the hall still wearing his underwear and socks.

Afraid that he might have talked while he was under the anesthetic, he asked the doctor what he'd said, as soon as he woke up after the operation. The doctor assured him that he had just mumbled, and that he hadn't paid any attention. When it was all over, John said the experience had given him an entirely new attitude toward patients and whatever pain they might suffer.

While John was recuperating, Ash Robinson distributed to the entire medical society a letter stating that "his former son-in-law wouldn't even pay for Joan's funeral but had spent lavish sums on his bride and her children." It was very embarrassing. Several people called John's office asking what in the world it was all about—and said how strange it was that they should be told something so personal. I had to tell John about it as soon as he came out of the anesthetic and was himself again, wanting to know what was going on at the office.

John was incensed. Ash was the one who had ordered a fancy funeral, so John's contention was that Ash could just pay the bill. Meanwhile we were at the hospital surrounded by the very people who had gotten the mailing.

Every time I left the house or returned, I saw Ash passing by. Frequently he spent entire afternoons waiting to see Robert. He became very chummy with Hedy, one of the nurses in John's office, and got quite a bit of inside information from her, including our unlisted telephone number. We started getting all kinds of calls.

"Dr. Hill, this is a reporter for *Newsweek*. I am here to do a story on Joan Robinson Hill's murder, and I suggest you give me an interview." John would turn purple and stammer, and say, "Well, uh, certainly." Then the appointment was never kept.

John was going crazy. One day he decided he and I would fly to New Orleans for the weekend, just to get away. We had to change our flight at the last minute, leaving final instructions with his office and my mother. We boarded the plane, and just as we were about to leave, one final passenger got on.

Ash Robinson!

He gave us a big smirk and sat behind us. If the plane hadn't been taxiing, I would have gotten off. John was quite nervous. Was he going to bump us off in mid-air? Did he have his Mafia connections in New Orleans set to do the deed?

When we landed, alive, I begged John to stay at the airport so we could take the next plane back to Houston, or anywhere. Ash was watching our every move and could hear almost every word we said.

How had he gotten our schedule? Only John's nurse and my mother knew, and I knew Mother hadn't told him! It must have been Hedy. I was way too upset to have a good time. Here we were trying to get away, and our troubles had followed us, literally!

When we got to our hotel, I had John inquire if Ash was registered there. He wasn't, but I felt only slightly relieved. We were taken to a penthouse, where there were no other occupants. I insisted we be changed to a busier part of the hotel, and that our room number *not* be given out. Then I had John phone the district attorney in Houston and express my concern, which he did. The district attorney was nice and said it probably was a coincidence that Ash Robinson was there also.

Then he added: "By the way, Dr. Hill, we can't find any problem with the will Joan left, naming her father beneficiary of her estate." John had asked the district attorney's office to examine a will, supposedly Joan's, that Ash had suddenly produced. Mr. Robinson claimed John thought Joan had died intestate and that he had hoped to inherit all of her estate. Sure enough, John didn't think there was a will, but then Ash took one to court and had it filed. It bequeathed "everything to her beloved parents, including the custody of Robert!" Of course, John unquestionably had legal custody of his own son. John was certain Ash had hastily authored the will, in Joan's name, but since he couldn't *prove* that Joan *hadn't* written it, it would have to stand.

That was all inconsequential as far as I was concerned. I was sure we wouldn't return to Houston alive. Ash had told half of the city he was going to "get even" with John. And I was pretty sure I wasn't on his list of favorite people. Every time he drove by our house, he glared at me.

We made it through the night, and the next morning John insisted we go across the street for brunch at Brennan's. Just as we walked in, we saw Ash leaving! He sort of ducked his head; I saw his face just as he turned around, and he looked sort of sheepish. We changed our scheduled flight back (it would not be the one John's nurse thought we were taking) and went home under an assumed name. You guessed it—Mr. and Mrs. J. R. Hyde. That old instinct just kept coming out—or whatever it was. Or was John subconsciously aware of being a real Jekyll and Hyde? I never was sure.

My life was so perplexing by then I scarcely noticed the daily routine (which was more than enough to keep me busy). It was as if our lives were being lived in italics, going from one major situation to another. If I hadn't inherited a tremendous ability to bounce back and a large portion of self-confidence from my parents, I never would have been able to endure those traumatic days. But that was the name of the game—endure.

I was struggling to keep going on the best of what we had together. Surely it would be enough to sustain us. I kept telling myself things would level off soon. If I could just get some time behind me. If only life could be like the old Cecil B. DeMille movies, where a calendar would flip the months by, and suddenly it would be *later,* and things would be *different*.

One day in October John brought home a bunch of Tyler roses, bought from a little boy on a corner. "They're my favorite kind," I said, and thanked him. He looked at me and said, "This time they're from me. Not from Jack." (He had recalled the time Jack Ramsay had sent the flower boy to my car with the same roses.) Our eyes met in remembrance of that day.

And then he told me: "Jack is dead, did you hear? He was in the hospital for a check-up. I noticed his name on a list of patients . . . Something strange and unexplainable appears to have caused his death."

I shuddered. I felt a sudden chill. But it wouldn't do to show any emotion or concern. Fortunately the maid interrupted, calling us to dinner, so no response or reaction was necessary.

What next? I just couldn't imagine that anything else would happen. I couldn't even get the nerve up to think it all through. There had to be an end to the wild roller-coaster ride I was on. One thing was certain: I wanted it to stop, and I wanted *out*. I couldn't help John. I couldn't change him. I couldn't ignore the facts. And unfortunately I couldn't change the facts or the situation. Now it appeared, I couldn't anticipate what he might do next. I felt certain that I was already living on borrowed time and must never cause him to think I would cross him, or my time would be up, too. I began to formulate definite plans to extricate myself from this captive state. One Sunday, when my boys were visiting their father, John and Robert and I went to a place on the bay for a seafood dinner. It was a nice treat for Robert to have all of our attention.

On the way home, Robert asked his dad if he could go to the horse farm sometime soon. He was quite a good rider and no doubt missed riding with his mother. John went into a complete tizzy and yelled and swerved the car crazily from one side to the other of the drawbridge we were crossing! (He wasn't too good a driver on bridges!)

Robert was screaming, cars were honking, and I finally grabbed and straightened the wheel. John must have realized he would be killed too, because he drove safely and in silence the rest of the way home. It was an incredible reaction to the mere mention of Robert's wanting to go riding! John was becoming terrifyingly unpredictable.

From that time on, Robert would never again ride in a car his father was driving. In fact, there were several scenes when he refused to go some place "unless Mom drives." Robert confessed that he was scared to death of his father. He said some of the children in the neighborhood had told him that his dad had been the one who made his mother die. It was difficult to give him any kind of reassurance at all. He often begged me to let him go see the Robinsons.

However, John was very firm in his decision that

Robert was never to see or talk to his grandparents, not even on the phone. I decided that Robert needed all the love and reassurance he could get, so I let him go over for a visit one day when I knew John was in surgery.

Mrs. Robinson was home alone, and she thought she was seeing things when Robert came in. Ash was out of town, and when he returned, he was certain his wife had had too much to drink and wasn't remembering, only wishing she had seen Robert. The next morning, the minute John drove out the drive, the phone rang. (Ash watched our every move.) As soon as he saw John leave, he went to a phone booth and called.

"Ann, this is Ash Robinson. Rhea tells me you let Robert come for a visit. I was out of town and she was all excited and crying and talking, and I couldn't believe her, but the maid says it's so. I just want you to know, if you ever did want to go to heaven, you can be sure of a place there now. That's the happiest I've ever seen Rhea, and you don't know how much we appreciate your sending little Robert down to our house."

I answered, "Yes, it was good for him, too—and he was sorry you were gone."

"Well, honey, I know I've given you a rough time. I've said some strong things against you, and I know I've scared those boys, just trying to catch a peek at Robert, but it's just because of this thing with John. We were awfully good to him, and he didn't do right by Joan. I'll talk to you another time about all this, but I was wondering if you could see your way clear to let me see little Robert."

I told him Robert would be over that afternoon as soon as I was sure John was in his office, but that John did not and must not know of the visit. He understood and was delighted. I thought all the more that John had made a terrible mistake in keeping Robert from seeing his grandparents. It was just bound to make them even more antagonistic toward him.

A few days later, when Robert was again going to see

the Robinsons, Ash asked if I would pick him up after a while and come in to visit for a minute. The Robinsons couldn't have been nicer or more appreciative. It seemed to bring some measure of peace to Robert's life, too.

Mr. Robinson said he had asked Robert, "Is she good to you?"

"Who, my new mom? Oh, yes! She's the best mom I ever had!"

We both chuckled over that. Ash asked me to sit down in the den. It was crowded with pictures of Joan and all of her trophies. He said, "Well, John had to give up on the will, didn't he?"

"I suppose so, yes."

He started telling me how good they had always been to John, and that nothing could have surprised them more than to have him turn so hostile as to forbid Robert to visit. "We loved John, and we were as good to him as if he were our own. But he wanted out—and when I crossed him, he destroyed my daughter's life. I know he did."

Ash contended that shortly before her death John had urged Joan to take out a large insurance policy (naming John beneficiary), and that Ash had successfully talked her out of it, pointing out that if anything happened to her, the Robinsons would be there to take care of Robert. Ash had not felt a costly policy was necessary. After Joan's death, he wondered all the more as he recalled John's insistence. He pressed me for details, asking if John ever confided in me about the circumstances of Joan's death. I said he hadn't, but that we weren't getting along very well, that I was trying to decide how to handle the situation, and that one of my real concerns was leaving Robert.

"Well, I don't know what's wrong with John," Ash said. "He's a strange one. I've heard more strange rumors about him than I care to remember."

Mrs. Robinson added: "Ann, do you mind if I ask you a personal question?"

"Rhea, now really," Ash interrupted.

"I don't mind, what is it?" I asked.

"Does John ever make love to you?"

"Oh, Rhea, of course you know he does."

"No, I don't know, Ash. I remember how distressed Joan used to be. One time she was upset and told me it had been eight or nine months since John had even touched her. Don't you consider that odd? I mean they were married, and you'd think, after all, he was young ... then another time, not too long before she died, she confided it had been more than a year and a half ..."

"Well, he and I were very happy at one point," I said, "but as I told your husband, things are just not working out. When there's a breakdown in a marriage, I guess that's the first thing to go, at least in a lot of cases. And no matter whose idea the abandonment might be, it's mighty awkward."

Ash Robinson continued, "You know, I've been awfully concerned about all you people. Most of all, Robert, of course, because John is capable of anything. I even talked to your former husband, Melvin, and told him he'd better keep an eye on his boys. He was very nice and most complimentary of you, by the way. I called him and he came over one evening. We chatted a while, and he said he had seen Robert with you and his boys recently, and that the boys were happy together and you were a good mother. He mentioned the fact that you had made a special effort to plan nice occasions for Robert, whenever his new brothers were going out with him. Rhea and I appreciate your taking such an interest in our little Robert. I guess in all the unhappiness, knowing he is happy and that you are good to him is about the best thing we've got going for us. I never could understand John's reason for keeping us from seeing our own grandson. Unless he had some ulterior motive. There's no telling what he did to poor Joan. Now that we have met, I'm distressed to know you are having problems. But I'm not surprised. I don't know exactly what it is, but there's something really wrong with John. His mother is a weird one, too."

I said we really must get back, but that Robert would be back in the next few days, and that he or I would call first. We went home, and John pulled in right behind us. Thank goodness he had come from the opposite direction and hadn't seen where Robert and I had been.

Robert visited on several occasions, and it always was a joyful time for him and his grandparents. I couldn't blame them for being upset with John, and wished there were some way to be certain Robert could be sure of continuing the visits. I have a strong feeling he sees them often, even now.

I could hardly believe that Melvin would talk to Ash Robinson, much less go to see him. Just how much could I believe of what this man said? After all, John was firm in his belief that Ash was a vindictive man who would stop at nothing to get even with John over the loss of his daughter. It only stood to reason that he must hate me as well. Certainly he had had me followed and stared and stared whenever he saw me. I had to find out from Melvin if there was indeed any truth to Mr. Robinson's conversation.

One Sunday, John, always the happy cheerleader of the family, suggested we take the boys to Astroworld. Robert refused to go unless I drove, so John agreed pleasantly enough, and we went to spend the day at the amusement park.

The children all knew the storm clouds were gathering over John's and my relationship. However they had no idea of the full extent of the problem, so we were always glad to resume our previous happy life, if only externally.

John was already getting on a ride with the boys when I declined at the last second and slipped away to a far corner of the amusement park and called Melvin. He confirmed what Mr. Robinson had told me. "But, Ann, be careful of him. I don't like that man. I was sorry as soon as I stepped inside his house. He called, sounding mysterious, and said he had some important matters to discuss with me regarding the boys. He insisted it was a life-and-death matter, and that I should talk with him immediately." He went on, "It was the strangest visit you could imagine, Ann. Mr. Robinson took me in a darkened room and started saying what a terrible person John is, and all about how he was positive he had had something to do with his daughter's death. I was sorry right away that I had even listened to him. He's just a pathetic person. I suggest you stay way away from him. He seems hell-bent on getting even some way. You don't know what a strange evening it was. I couldn't get out of there fast enough. But he just kept talking. I think he thought I might chime in and say how much I didn't like my ex-wife, or her new husband, or something. I guess he was disappointed, if that's what he expected, because I assured him that you are the greatest mother in the world, and that the boys, including Robert, were very happy, and I even mentioned that John seemed to be devoted to his family. Anyway, I'm sorry I ever talked to the man. You're okay, aren't you? I mean, there's nothing to what he says, is there? He was just adamant in his feeling about John. He even called him a murderer."

"Well, Melvin, uh, John and I are coming to a parting of the ways . . ." I stammered.

"Good Lord! Mr. Robinson isn't right about John, is he? I mean John didn't really kill Joan or anything . . . *did he?*"

"I don't know what to think about John," I said. "Except that he's not what I thought he was, and I don't know what to do about it. I feel so concerned about Robert. That's why I let him see his grandparents, even though John disapproves and doesn't know that Robert and I have both seen the Robinsons."

I must have been on the phone for thirty minutes when one of the boys spotted me in the phone booth. I had to hang up quickly. John was with them, heading toward me.

"Melvin, I've got to hang up. Thank you for telling me. I really didn't know whether to believe Mr. Robinson or not."

"Ann, don't hang up. Tell me, is there anything to all this? I mean, if there is, don't stop to think about *how:* just *leave.* You and the boys just get away from him. My God, don't take any chances with your lives if John is some kind of a kook."

John opened the door to the phone booth. "Baby, we've looked all over for you! Who are you talking to?"

I knew I looked confused. What to say? How to explain? I said into the phone, "Oh, here they are now! Well, the boys will see you *next* Sunday then, if it's okay, and I'm sorry about today, Melvin, I just completely forgot till we got to Astroworld that they were supposed to see you today. Bye!"

"Well, I guess we just got separated," I explained. "Where have you been? I went to the ladies' room, and when I came out, you had already left the ride you were on when I saw you last. Then I remembered you boys were supposed to get together with Melvin today. So I called him to explain. You can get together next week, okay?" I asked the boys.

With the children and the confusion, I knew John would probably believe my explanation, and certainly he'd never check with Melvin. Melvin seemed to have a grasp of the situation, to say the least.

How was I going to get away? It always *sounds* so simple. "I'll just leave him! I won't stand still for one moment longer in this mess. I'll just go." I told myself. But how could I, really? John was watching me like a hawk. He had even begun picking up the phone and listening in on my conversations. What I needed to do was just approach it from a no-argument standpoint.

No reasons, just the statement. "Let's plan to separate," I would say. No problems. Still friends. Surely I could take that approach. As Scarlett said, "I'll worry about that tomorrow." Except that I also had to worry about the rest of the day, then that night, and hope to God there would *be* a tomorrow.

I drove us all home, and it was good to hear the boys bubbling over their afternoon adventures. John and I would just have to have a talk. At least I could feel him out on the subject. I must remember not to get weepy or upset or mention Joan, or any other upsetting incidents. I couldn't continue as I was, waiting for something to happen. I'd be lucky if nothing else *did* happen.

It was time for me to turn the situation in a direction that I could handle. I desperately needed a way out, a way to put this nightmare behind me forever. The episode on the bridge with Robert was really the last straw. I went to speak to an attorney about a divorce (without John's knowledge).

My attorney listened politely while I explained that "the marriage just isn't working out." He had been employed by Ash Robinson shortly after Joan's death to find out what had happened to Joan. He was quite familiar with the case, and asked me if I felt that John was responsible for Joan's death. I avoided answering him directly, and said something to the effect that John was upset, I was upset, the Robinsons were upset, and I didn't know how to make an exit, particularly because of Robert.

He asked me just how much John had told me about the situation. I said, "John said he never even went to the cemetery after Joan's funeral, and as far as he was concerned, he wanted the entire subject closed right there, because, after all, Joan was gone."

My attorney said, "I am afraid I must acquaint you with some of the facts in the matter. For a *fact,* Dr. Hill indeed returned to the cemetery following Joan's funeral. I have, personally, seen a court order signed by Dr. Hill *requesting that Joan's body be exhumed for the purpose of removing a ring!"*

I couldn't believe it. I was incredulous as he continued. "Then, one rainy, misty evening shortly after the funeral, John and *some woman* went to the cemetery at closing time with the court order. The workers were preparing to leave. John told them to just *remove the casket,* and he would take care of the rest. The workers *opened the grave, removed the casket,* and rolled it to an adjacent area, then left for the day. Did he ever mention this to you?"

I was aghast! It was like the worst part of a horror movie where everybody looks down at the floor and says, "Tell me when it's over"—yet this was John he was talking about.

"It *couldn't* be so!" I said. I had suggested to John once, on Mother's Day, that he should take Robert to the cemetery. John was emphatically against the idea. "I've never been to the cemetery since the funeral, and I don't ever plan to go there," he had said.

My attorney said he had made inquiries at the cemetery, and that no one knew what had happened, only that the body was apparently reburied, as the grave was covered over when they returned the next day.

I was limp. The idea was just *unthinkable.* Why? What would John have had Joan's body exhumed for? What had he *done?* Then I remembered the envelope from the funeral home that said "Mrs. Hill's ring," locked away in John's closet. The funeral home had obviously *given* John the ring, so *that* wasn't why he had had her body removed.

Then my attorney suggested that I read a deposition taken from Joan's maid, Effie Green. It was a ghastly description of Joan's illness, and John's apparent lack of care and concern. Those last tortured hours had left a vivid impression on Effie:

SUMMARY OF DEPOSITION OF EFFIE GREEN

During Tuesday morning Mrs. Hill had uncontrollable diarrhea and was so weak she couldn't walk to the bathroom alone. Her condition grew progressively worse. ·

Dr. Hill called her into their bedroom early that morning and told her to "clean up the mess."

Putting Mrs. Hill back in bed, she said she discovered the bedding and three towels put under Mrs. Hill were fouled and stained with blood. She said she cleaned up the bed.

The maid said that the second time she was walking Mrs. Hill back to bed "she told me that she couldn't hardly see."

This time, Effie said, Mrs. Hill was dragging one of her feet, and her head lolled to one side. She said she was "burning from her stomach up."

The maid testified that after Mrs. Hill was back in bed after the third trip to the bathroom, "she stretched herself out and pushed herself back" in a sort of spasm.

"I thought she was about to pass," Effie said.

By this time, she said, Mrs. Hill was turning purplish or blue around her cheeks and lips.

"I prayed with her," the maid said.

She said she urged Mrs. Hill to go to a hospital, and she nodded a "yes." She then telephoned and left word for Dr. Hill to hurry home, she said, while her husband summoned the dying woman's parents.

She was questioned as to whether Dr. Hill at any time picked his wife up and carried her downstairs (as he had contended). "No sir, Dr. Hill said, 'She can make it, let her walk.'"

It was sickening. My flesh was crawling. It was getting late, and of all things it was Halloween. I told the attorney that I must be leaving, but that I would be back in touch. John didn't know of my appointment. As I drove home, I was unable to think of anything but the strange unsettling things I had learned about my husband.

John drove in just as I had changed my clothes; he had no idea I had been gone, much less to an attorney. We went downstairs to a late dinner. The boys were busy trick-or-treating. The doorbell rang constantly with little goblins. My nerves were shot, but I couldn't ignore the things I had learned. To this day I can't believe my *nerve*.

"John," I said, "you should know by now you aren't invisible."

"What, baby?"

"When you and *some woman* went to the cemetery, a few days after Joan's funeral, and had her *body removed,* it didn't go *unnoticed!*"

John finished a bite, carefully wiped his mouth, and looked at me levelly. "Who told you that? There's no one in the world who could have told you that. Nobody saw us."

"I thought you said you had no desire to return to the cemetery. But you *did,* with *some woman*. Why in the *world* did you do that?"

"Oh, I don't know," he said calmly, "just something I thought best to do at the time."

"And who was the woman?"

"Of course, that would have to have been my mother."

Perfectly calm.

He didn't even ask me again how I had heard it.

I think by then he was beginning to have doubts about his mind, and thought I was something of a mind reader. He couldn't figure it out.

And the things I had figured out I couldn't cope with.

He knew I was completely turned off of him. What an awkward time it was.

John became more and more concerned that a grand jury was supposedly reconsidering an indictment against him in Joan's death. He was frantic because he had no attorney to handle the case, or even to consult with. I asked an attorney friend to recommend a criminal lawyer for John. His response was, "My God, if he thinks he needs a criminal lawyer, he must know. Are you all right?"

When contacted for an appointment, the attorney John was referred to said he had "heard rumblings from the grand jury that they were thinking about indicting him for Murder One." That really put the fear in him!

(Months later the district attorney said that was completely untrue, they weren't even thinking of John Hill at that time. They simply had come to a dead end. He suggested that the attorney had literally scared John into acting in a way that made him more suspect.)

Richard (Racehorse) Haynes, the attorney who John called, came over late one night to visit. He heard John's version, heavily laced with intimations of the facts. ("I don't know why everyone thinks something was wrong with some pastries I served Joan. There is no poison I could have given her that wouldn't be traceable. Her father seems to hold me accountable for her death." He was practically spilling the whole story.) Mr. Haynes sat there watching John and listening. His expression revealed considerable insight into the situation, every time John touched on one of those obvious "near confessions."

"Well," said the lawyer, "as I see it, the grand jury will be looking at two points. Motive"—and he stopped and looked at me—"and opportunity." He got up to leave, and John was stunned. Here the man had heard his story, saw his need, and was getting up to leave without suggesting the possibility of any help.

"There's no way I can defend you, John, as long as you are so happily ensconced with so obvious a motive." (That is, as long as he was living with me.) He suggested John might call him at his office the next day and they would continue the discussion.

John was really in a dilemma. He was more concerned than ever that he was facing certain indictment, and now the highly recommended criminal attorney was refusing to take the case unless John would disengage himself from our marriage. John suggested we could divorce and remarry after he was in the clear. I suggested we could divorce, period.

"Oh come on, baby, I'll make you decide you can never leave me. I do need to get some cash together to be ready to make bond. Let's see, I have about $4,000 in my downtown checking account," and he listed several amounts in various accounts.

"How much can you get your hands on, baby? I guess it's lucky your house sold. When is the closing set? We'll need that $15,000 profit you've got coming. Racehorse tells me his fee will be $10,000 for starters, and if I'm indicted for Murder One, then he'll take everything I've got."

It was a bad time. I was totally finished with John after the second bridge scare. I had refused to sleep with him after that episode, and that made for a difficult situation. He had begun an eerie night-time routine. He would go to the music room and play the piano or stereo till two or three in the morning. Our whole lives seemed to be played to the background of John's favorite music by Mozart and Rachmaninoff.

One night when I walked into the music room, he was playing a tape and listening so intently that he didn't notice me when I came in. It was Joan's voice, a taped conversation of her begging John to reconcile.

"John," I cried, "what in the world are you doing? If Robert heard that, it would surely upset him."

"I have lots of tapes like this." (He was editing it then.) "I can make her say anything I want to. It might be useful someday, if ever there is a trial."

I sat down and said, "John, let's just discuss what's

going to happen, and decide pleasantly what's the best way to handle the situation happily for everyone. This can't go on and on."

I told him I just wanted to be back where I was when he met me. (Unfortunately, my house had just been sold, but I could find another.) John urged me to hold off on any plans to terminate our marriage. He wanted to plan a day off that week and go to Galveston or somewhere and talk things out to see if we could come up with a happy way to reconcile. As he pointed out, he was happy, and if it was the last thing he did, he was going to make me love him the way he loved me. "That's something that won't die, baby. Not ever."

John had put in a gorgeous pool in the backyard. The gossip columns ran every item they could on the "interesting doctor," complete with the price of the pool he had built for his stepsons. It was next to impossible to maintain a happy carefree atmosphere for the children. I was "on guard" every minute John was around.

When he left for hospital rounds one evening, the boys and I decided to go for a swim. John returned unexpectedly, sent the boys in to bed, and stripped and jumped into the pool with me. He was being very sweet and cuddly. He held me in his arms and looked at me. "Isn't this romantic? This is the way I wish I could always be with my baby."

A sickening feeling came over me. Nobody could see or hear us. I had a terrible premonition that I was about to "accidentally drown," even though I was a better swimmer than John. We weren't swimming, he was just holding me. Mindful that my best approach was to be tender and loving, I snuggled up to him and said, "This would be a lot more fun if the water were just a little warmer. Why don't you turn up the thermostat?" Always a gentleman, John got out to adjust the temperature.

I got out fast. "Brrr, I'm freezing," and I ran into the house. He knew I had sensed impending disaster, but he never mentioned my speedy exit.

I tried to stay surrounded by the children, but there were always times when John managed for us to be alone. I was becoming physically exhausted. I couldn't sleep when he was there, so I'd nap in the daytime when he left. My weight had dropped about twenty pounds, and my family and friends were beginning to question me about my health. Far from being the radiant bride, I was beginning to look like a ghost of my former self. I was on a tightrope. It wasn't safe at home with him, and I didn't know how to get away.

We went to the symphony, surrounded by acquaintances, several of whom later remarked to Ash that "John sat there the whole time with both his arms around her. I thought you said they were breaking up. They must have reconciled." The next morning the paper said we were "happy newlyweds, enjoying each other more than the symphony."

Two days later the same reporter said, "All is not well with Ann and John Hill; they're telling it to the judge, our spies tell us." That was all I needed. Now my every thought was being reported to the world. I guess Ash was too overjoyed over our "problems" to keep it to himself. John was furious. How could anyone say such a thing. He would show them. We were to go to lunch at the Doctors Club and they would see how happy we were.

During this period, John was engrossed with a fascinating accident case on which he was to do reconstructive surgery. A man's face had been virtually destroyed in a terrible fire. The family had produced photographs so that he might be restored, as nearly as possible, to his former self. Through his agony and pain, the man begged John not to reproduce his former features. "Doc," he said, "I've been a failure all my life. I want a new face and a new chance to be the person I know I can be. Please help me, sir. I want to have a chance with the rest of my life. I want to go out of this place a new man."

John was determined to help him. In medical school, he had often performed plastic surgery at a prison outside Houston specifically to change certain facial characteristics. A number of the men had shown entirely different attitudes once some disfiguring feature was altered to a more pleasant appearance.

Now John was faced with the opportunity of creating a complete new face for someone. The man's family showed absolutely no sign of recognition when they saw the patient after his bandages were removed. The man returned later and said his entire outlook on life had changed. It was like being reborn in the middle of a lifetime. John later said it was his most challenging and rewarding case.

All this time, I felt an overwhelming concern for Robert. He was so lovable and so confused and afraid. John seemed to have an intense dislike for his own son. He commented frequently and bitterly about Robert's striking resemblance to his mother! I was afraid John would look at him one day and become his other dreadful self.

He couldn't stand any mention of horses, or bear to see any pictures of Joan. He habitually turned face-down a photo of Joan and Robert that was by Robert's bed. He had made an unsettling scene in that regard, when I was at his office. I had gone to meet him for lunch, and he pulled me into a seldom used examining room for a quick hug. I became aware of him growing rigid. I pulled back and saw he was staring at a picture on the wall behind me. It was Joan on her famous horse, Beloved Belinda. You would have thought Joan herself had walked into the room. He pulled the picture down without a word, ripped off the frame, and carried the photo into the bathroom where he tore it into a thousand pieces and flushed it in the toilet.

Another time, he assembled all of Joan's trophies, ribbons, photos, and mementos, everything belonging to her that was still at his house, and made a bonfire of them in the barbecue pit. He was becoming increasingly unpredictable. His moods fluctuated rapidly and without any warning or reason.

John frequently brought up the idea of moving. "Baby, couldn't we begin again in Mexico? I know a lot of people there, and they are in great need of plastic surgeons in that country. I could set up a practice in Mexico City, and we could lead a brand-new life. No memories to haunt us. No people from the past to surround us. I'll check on requirements to practice there. I'm sure it's a mere formality. Wouldn't that be a happy solution?"

I hated to burst his bubble of optimism, but I honestly couldn't think of going anywhere with him. It was too late. I had to be honest with him and told him that it wouldn't help.

I had noticed that Robert was particularly fond of a fluffy white Pomeranian puppy that we had gotten for the boys. Whenever I saw him hugging the dog, I realized all over again how much love and reassurance he needed. Lots of times at night I would open his door and let the puppy sleep with him. It was our special little secret.

One day the maid came running upstairs. There was a horrible commotion in our side yard. John and I ran down, and, to our horror, saw a huge Dalmatian, which had already killed several small dogs in the neighborhood, devouring the puppy! We turned on the hose and drove the big dog away, but it was too late for the Pomeranian.

The owner of the Dalmatian was most upset when we told her of the incident. She had inadvertently trained the dog to kill the wrong thing. One day she had jokingly pointed to a squirrel and said, "Kill." The dog was a fast learner. But there was one problem: there was a white poodle directly behind the squirrel, and that's what the dog focused his attention on. The tragic result was that the Dalmatian was now programmed to kill white fluffy dogs. Ours was the fifth one in the neighborhood to meet such a fate.

The children came home from school and were heartbroken to learn their dog had been killed. The yardman had taken care of the burial, and right away the boys and I went to all the pet stores until we found a suitable replacement. I just couldn't let Robert endure another grief, and the old custom of "getting a new puppy" seemed the best solution. How can you really explain away the hurt of something like that to a child? I felt that Robert had been through more than any one nine-year-old should be expected to suffer.

Shortly after that incident I was standing at the window, watching the Dalmatian stalking the neighborhood. John asked me what I was doing. "Just watching that killer. Why does he do it? Can't somebody retrain him? Can't they teach him what he does is wrong? He just walks up and down the street all day, and whenever he takes the notion he attacks and kills again. How could we live in such a nice neighborhood, and just sit here, knowing there's a *killer* out there?"

John was standing beside me. I looked up and noticed a nerve twitching in his cheek. Oh, good heavens! He had thought I was talking about *him*. Glancing at the dog, John said, "I really don't think he can help it. It's something he was programmed to do, and he probably couldn't stop if he tried."

Was he speaking for himself as well?

All this time, John's attorney was calling with countless rumors, keeping him in a state of near hysteria. "They'll probably indict you next Wednesday or Thursday," his lawyer told him. So John decided we would go to Galveston on Wednesday.

That Tuesday John was depressed and morose. He asked me to meet him at the office and said we'd go out to dinner before time to make rounds. I was waiting for John to finish and saw a note on his desk, addressed to me.

I opened it.

Last Will and Testament: I love my sweet darling.
John

My God! He was planning to take his life! John came in and saw me reading the note. I was in tears. He came over and hugged me. "Oh baby, I'm sorry you saw that. I was just so depressed. You do love me. It's all right."

"John, what did you mean? What were you *thinking?* That's no answer!"

"Baby, I could handle it. I could be walking down the hall of a hospital and make it look like I just had a heart attack."

"Don't, John, remember we're going to have a happy day tomorrow."

It was a sad and tender moment. We clung together, knowing it was hopeless. Wanting something that was, but could never again be. Where had it gone? How could all the love we shared be lost? I had no answers. And really no hope. Nothing. I was *drained*.

The next morning we left home early, and shortly after our departure I noticed we were heading for East Texas. (Yes, I was nervous to be going anywhere with him. We were sure to cross many bridges, and I couldn't put his "bad driving record" out of my mind.)

He decided we would go to Hodges Gardens at the edge of Louisiana instead. That sounded fine (at least we would miss crossing that long causeway to Galveston!). We stopped for breakfast in Beaumont, and John was sweet and happy. He reached across the table and squeezed my hand. "I love you so. Everyone can see that. Those people at the next table probably think we're on our honeymoon! How did I get so lucky to find you? That's right, I went to camp! It's like I always heard, 'There's nothing better for a boy than a summer camp'—and it wasn't bad for me either!"

He stopped me outside, on the way to the car, and took some pictures. "I want to remember today—always." John was in a reminiscent mood. He recounted some particularly tender moments between us; everything was bittersweet.

As we proceeded toward Louisiana, another of those strange moods came over him. He started talking just the way he did the night when he told me about what had happened to Joan.

"You know, baby, sometimes there comes a time when some people are no longer meant for this world." Did he mean me? He had my complete attention. Truthfully, I was thinking of how I might jump out of my side of the car.

"Actually," he continued, "there are several strange and sudden deaths I have been associated with!" He seemed very proud.

"Oh, honestly, John," I said. "Luckily a plastic surgeon doesn't handle life-and-death cases. You just make people beautiful! Aren't you glad? And it must make you awfully proud when you do some of your reconstructive surgery."

Not to be deterred, he interrupted, his voice taking on that peculiarly dreadful tone I had heard before. "Well, there was my brother, Julian. Of course, it appeared to be suicide. I was the last person with him. We had such a delightful evening; we played piano duets." His face was indescribably changed as he continued, "Then later when they found him, he had taken an overdose of morphine. He was slumped by the piano, with the score turned to our favorite duet. Quite a fitting gesture, I thought."

Good God! I had cold chills.

He went on, "Then, my father passed on shortly after my brother. He had been asking so many questions about Julian. He had a heart condition, so when he died a few weeks later, everyone just assumed it was from a heart attack. I had prescribed some medication that was certain to be fatal to a man in his condition."

There was a real smirk on his face.

"Then, of course, there was Joan . . ."

Realizing that he wouldn't be telling me this if he expected me to live with the knowledge, I became very nervous. "Well, that's all in the past, John. Let's just have a nice day."

Not to be diverted, he continued: "Then there was my good friend Andrew Gordon."

"Oh, yes," I remembered, "he's the doctor friend you told me about who committed suicide a few years ago."

"Well"—with a smile—"they never did figure that one out. They just knew he died from an overdose of something. We were together that afternoon. He and I had been very close, but he had become very jealous of me. Then, there was . . ." The weird conversation broke off.

We were approaching Hodges Gardens. The gatekeeper came out, noticed the car, and said, "Are you Dr. John Hill? Your attorney has been calling, looking for you all morning. He said for you to call him at his office in Houston as soon as you got here. There's a phone."

John was in such a nervous sweat he could hardly dial. When he reached his lawyer, he was very noncommittal. "All right, that's all right, well, I'm sure you did what you thought was best. No, Richard, I'll get it all worked out, I'll start back right away."

His face was white. I asked him to let me drive. "No, I'll be all right. Just let me think."

"Please tell me what he said," I begged.

"Well, baby, they have indicted me. I'll probably be incarcerated tomorrow."

I was stunned. "John, please pull in by that little church. Let's go in, just for a minute. Let's just gather our strength and then we can better analyze the situation and decide what's best to do."

Really, I had in mind what he might do when we came to the next bridge. Would that seem like a good solution to him? It had been part of his "modus operandi" before. "Let me drive," I offered.

"No, baby, we must hurry home. We need to plan things. You'll need to bring my dictating equipment to me," and he went on with plans for the children's and my welfare while he was "away."

"And we'll have to assemble all our cash for me to make the necessary bail. It will take quite a large sum, Mr. Haynes tells me. Your house should close soon enough to pledge that $15,000 profit. And how much is in your checking accounts?" I told him I had been to the banks I did business with, after he had mentioned needing cash, and that I had already assembled several thousand dollars at the house.

I thought he was going to cry! "Oh, baby! You do love me!" He put his arms around me. "We'll work it out."

Shortly, thereafter, we arrived at a filling station, and while the car was being serviced, I said I would call and see if the boys had all gotten home from school. John tried to tell me we didn't have time, but I was already dialing.

My father answered! He was at John's and my house; I knew he was to have gone to Los Angeles on business that day.

"Papa! What's going on? I thought you were on a trip? Are the boys okay? Did you hear about John?"

"Ann, it's you! Good Lord!" (There was a catch in his voice.) "I've tried every way in the world to locate you. The sheriff's department is looking everywhere along the Galveston highway. Where are you? Are you all right?" He was really broken up.

Then he hastened to say, "Listen to me, Ann, don't let on, don't say a word, just listen to me. Right after you left, the maid called us and said John's attorney had come to the house, and a moving van had pulled up, and the attorney said he was there to supervise 'moving Mrs. Hill's and her children's things back to her house.'"

Of course, the maid knew the house was sold, and certainly I would have mentioned such a plan if I were moving, so she had called my parents, and Papa had canceled his trip. He told John's lawyer who he was, and that if he didn't get out of his daughter's house, he would call the law. Finally, the attorney sent the van away and left. He had even gone to Robert's school and tried to have Robert released to him, but the principal became alarmed and would not permit Robert to leave with someone he did not know. Later that afternoon Mrs. Hill went to get Robert, and the teacher informed her that Robert would not be permitted to leave except with his mother. Robert's teacher had been my fourth-grade teacher. John was watching me as I listened to what Papa was telling me had transpired in our absence.

"Let me talk to John," Papa said. I handed him the telephone.

"All right, John, I don't want to go into all of this on the phone, but I want you to bring Ann home, and we will be waiting. I want you to know that if there is any problem, or any 'accident' is on your agenda, it had better happen to me first, because if anything happens to Ann, then whatever happens to you will be no accident. Do you understand?"

"Oh, yes, Cameron, certainly. How very nice of

you and Helen to be there with the boys. You have nothing to worry about. I love and cherish Ann and the boys. I'm sure we can iron this little episode out. I'm afraid my attorney acted in an unfortunate manner. I assure you there will be no problem. We will be there shortly. Thanks again."

When we got back to the car, I couldn't decide, as I told John, whether to be more relieved he hadn't really been indicted (that story was just to distract me) or more infuriated over his attorney's idea of making the separation and divorce he had prescribed for the doctor easier.

John was filled with remorse. "I have been the recipient of some very bad advice from my attorney. I swear if you will forget this, I'll retain another lawyer and spend the rest of my life being with you the way I was before I got embroiled in all of this."

We talked about how it could ever be the same. I didn't want to bring up all the nightmares I could never forget, so I assured him that there would be no reference to anything he had ever said or done. I just wanted to get home alive.

He was so concerned about my father that he stopped at a roadside phone booth and called him again. "Cameron? I trust the maid has served you and the boys dinner. It's raining, so of course we have to drive slowly, but I want to reassure you that we will be along in just about an hour."

Papa said, "Fine, we'll have your dinner waiting; thank you for calling. May I speak to Ann, please?" (My father was just checking to see if his daughter was still all right.) John handed me the phone.

"Ann, now don't go into all of this. Remember the important thing is for you to get home. Then everything else can be handled. Remember the old saying, 'Don't plug any melons.' " (Meaning: Don't plunge into anything when you don't know its contents.)

As we got to our house and saw Papa's car, John

turned off the ignition and pulled me close to him. "Don't betray me, Ann. Whatever I said to you is between us. Your father seems to think you will come to some harm with me. I want you to go inside and reassure him that we can work this matter out ourselves, and he need not be concerned. I love you so much, baby. I'm really glad Racehorse's [his lawyer] plan was foiled. I don't care if he won't represent me. We can make it together, can't we?" He smothered me with kisses. He was really nervous about facing Papa.

We went inside and John again reassured my father that it had been a most unfortunate misunderstanding. "Would you care to stay the night? No? Well, we'll be in touch first thing in the morning. I'm determined to show you and Ann that any worries you may have are groundless."

He refused to leave me alone with Papa and hurriedly rushed my parents out to their car, urging me to check on the boys. I nodded to Papa that I would be fine, and he announced that he would be back early the next morning on his way to the office.

The next morning Papa arrived as I was in the kitchen making coffee. We had a moment together before John came downstairs. My father expressed his anxiety for me. The previous day had more than shown him that there was something drastically wrong with his son-in-law. I told my father I was planning to see my attorney that day, and I urged him not to worry.

Just as John was sitting down to breakfast, the doorbell rang. It was his mother: she had arrived bag and baggage. As she put her things down in the entry hall, John said, "I wondered where you were. Racehorse said you were here yesterday, but we were away."

"Mr. Haynes told me you are about to be indicted for Joan's death. Is that so?"

"Well, that's what he seems to think."

"John, remember, it says in Ecclesiastes 'There is

wickedness in the place of justice.' I am here to comfort you. No one understands these things but you and I, son. Lord knows you had your reasons when it came to Joan. 'For everything there is a season.' I have told you before, there comes a time when some people are no longer meant for this world. You and I understand these things. They were only obstacles to be eliminated. God speaks to me and you know I hear His message. 'A time to build, and a time to cast away.' Now you must cast away this woman, John. Truly, truly I say to you, she will betray you."

Papa and I were in the kitchen. John's mother made no attempt to conceal her advice from us. My father and I exchanged uneasy glances as we heard John say: "Please, Mother. I will handle this my own way. I want Ann to forgive my transgressions. I need her and cherish her. Please understand."

"No, John. 'What has been is what will be, and what has been done is what will be done."

Papa and I walked through the hall and nodded hello to Mrs. Hill; I said I would be back later, and left with Papa. I still wasn't dressed for the day, but I had to get out. We drove around and talked until we saw John had left for the office. I called and made an appointment to see my attorney, but he was tied up in court for the next two days. Fortunately, my friend Joyce was arriving for a visit, and that gave me a good excuse to spend a lot of time with her. At least I wouldn't be left alone with John.

As if I hadn't had enough to contend with, there now were all these other "strange and sudden" deaths John had told me about. My emotional state had reached hurricane proportions. Whether I was shopping or at a friend's, he was calling on the phone or buzzing me on my paging device. It got to the point where I couldn't get anything done for the interruptions. My friends were incredulous over his constant calls.

John was still sending flowers, still trying to make me forget. Even later, after I filed for divorce, the flowers came and always with a timely and appropriate personal note. His constant lament was, "Baby, if only I hadn't told you. I should have realized what your reaction would be. Please, darling, it was the only way to keep from losing you. I couldn't bear that then, and I still can't even think of life without you. I won't stop at anything to have your love."

We went to the symphony, as always. John had sent me a beautiful bouquet of flowers, and two white orchids to wear one night. My parents were there for dinner, and as we were leaving, John said, "Isn't she beautiful? Here, wear your flowers, honey"—and he pinned them on me. "I want everyone to know you are mine."

Mother and Daddy watched, and when John went to get the car, Papa said, "Ann"—and suddenly choked up and turned away. He was weeping.

"Papa?"

"Just be careful. I know he loves you, but I can't explain it, I just have this feeling. *Please,* please be careful . . ."

So much had happened. There was so much he sensed but hadn't been told, so much he instinctively understood about the sad sad look in his daughter's eyes. But what had put it there? What was wrong? I knew he was worried. So was I, but I was the one who had to handle it. There had to be a way out of the situation, without encountering any more of John's determination to play God when people went against his wishes.

I felt this was as good a time as any to tell John of my plans. I had to begin somewhere. We were in the garden admiring a fountain he had had installed. The occasion was reminiscent of happier days spent in a similar spot at my home.

"John, let's sit down and have a heart-to-heart talk," I said.

He looked at me closely. "What is it, baby?"

We gazed steadily at each other, as I continued. "John, you know as well as I do that I am at the breaking point. Neither of us would deny that ours has been the great love of a lifetime, for each of us. I don't want to hurt you, or to wrong you in any way. But I do know myself, John, and I know that if we continue as we are, we are on a collision course with disaster. Without diminishing the great love we have known, I want us to take a step that I feel is the right one at this time. And that is to move apart. We are no longer in tune with one another. Let's not drag it on until we destroy what we have had together. No one can take that away from us."

Everything was blurred by the tears that filled my eyes. As I blinked, John traced a falling tear down my cheek. His voice was choked as he took my face in both his hands. I kissed them and cried, "My God, John! Why did this happen? I can't stand it—I think I'm going to disintegrate with unhappiness. Our beautiful world together has exploded all around us, and if we don't take a drastic step, we'll be destroyed—totally. I'll never be the same, John. I'll never ever even think of love without it being you. No one could ever be what you were to me. But I *have* to leave. I *have* to find some sanity. I *have* to find a quiet world of my own, where I can be whatever is left for me to be. All I want is to take my boys back where they will feel at home. They sense all of this, and they deserve better from me."

John looked down at me as he held me tenderly. "Ann, I know the state you are in. It kills me to see those eyes that used to sparkle clouded with the hurt I've caused you. I could remove the frown, or take a little tuck and put a smile on your mouth. But what I can't seem to do is rekindle the flame deep within you.

I know I've put it out. I know each and every thing that I have said and done to turn you off. I just kept hoping I could turn your love on again.

"Will you come to me if you ever feel it returning? Will you call me wherever, whenever it happens? Even if you wake up in the middle of the night and realize that you want me again—and know that all I want is to be with you—will you call me and let me come to you? Will you promise you will never consciously *try* to snuff out the faintest flicker of love, if it should begin to return?"

"Yes, John, I promise. I could never deny that to you. This isn't a happy feeling for me, you know. It's cold and lonely and sad."

We were interrupted by the boys, who had come out for a swim, and we turned our attention to them.

A couple of days before we planned to separate, we spent what we both knew would be our last evening together. It was a very sad "countdown." John planned to be home for dinner at six. We both pulled in the driveway at six-fifteen, and laughed when we said at the same time, "Sorry I'm late." Then, again simultaneously, we each handed the other a record. Both of us were late because we had gone to get a record, an appropriate message, for the other. I had gotten "With Pen in Hand." John wept when he played it, and I'm sobbing eight years later as I write about it. He brought me "The Windmills of Your Mind." Most fitting.

Shortly after, John refused to leave as he had promised, until I moved into another house. I had more conferences with my attorney. He knew I was afraid of John, but he didn't know why. Finally my lawyer arranged for a preliminary divorce hearing. As John and I stood before the judge and answered questions, my attorney said, "Mrs. Hill, Dr. Hill's attorney contends you have a cruel and unforgiving temper, is this so?"

That hit a nerve, and I responded automatically: "No, I think I've been very understanding and forgiving, considering that he has terrified me and tried to kill me."

It was just my immediate response to the question, but it landed like a bomb in the court, where reporters were already curiously gathering to see why the doctor and his bride were getting a divorce—especially since there was still so much controversy about the way his first wife had died.

That day the judge ordered John to take temporary residence elsewhere until I could relocate in my old neighborhood, as was my wish. When John came home that night he made no mention of what I had blurted out in court, in spite of the fact that it had made the front page of the paper. Two deputy sheriffs were waiting to serve papers on him, to the effect that he was under court order to vacate the premises until I could relocate myself and the boys. He read the court order, gave them a searing glance, then with a winning smile said, "Certainly, gentlemen, I'll just have a word with my wife and get my things." They indicated they would be outside waiting.

His time had run out. John had no way of avoiding our farewell now. He had tried to convince both our attorneys that we could live together until I chose to move to another house. Now he was being forced to leave; two very imposing-looking deputies were there to see that the court order was carried out. My parents were also there, as well as a private detective I had employed for the past several days as a bodyguard, just in case John got any more ideas about any more "strange and sudden deaths he might be closely associated with."

John came into the room, put both arms around me, and said, "Darling, when I saw you in court it was all I could do to keep from putting my arms around you like this. You know, you look better right now than I've ever seen you." (At that moment, all I could think of was that he had said Joan looked better in her coffin than he'd ever seen her.)

"We never did get to have that little girl we wanted," he continued. "Please, baby, stop all this. We can start all over again. Everything that happened was because I couldn't bear for us to be apart. I can't bear it now or ever. Go tell your folks and that guard and the deputies to leave, and let's be together, happily ever after."

My eyes filled with tears. Here was the person I had loved so deeply, but who I now knew had the capacity to turn into a monster, yet all the while so cunningly resembling my beloved John. I really had to fight against all my instincts—a part of me wanting to believe what he was saying, wishing we could turn back and find ourselves the way we used to be. But the overwhelming fear I had come to know was powerful and all-consuming.

I looked at him and said: "John, when you said 'till death do us part,' I didn't know you meant you would choose the time and the place." As I finished speaking, my father walked into the room and reminded John, in a very polite way, that he should be leaving.

When John tried to get his son to leave, there was a horrible episode: Robert ran away. We looked all over the neighborhood for him, and finally the police called. The nine-year-old child had gone to a service station and requested someone to please look up a judge in the telephone book for him. They had called the police discreetly, and a friendly officer was sent to see the little boy. Robert insisted on seeing a judge to ask "if he could stay with his new mother, because he was afraid of his father." He was taken to the police station and questioned. It didn't take them too long to figure out who he was. They called, and I went to get Robert, urging John to let him stay at the house till we moved.

John's mother turned up about that time, very much

on her high horse, saying she needed to have Robert with her so she could "train him in the ways of the Lord" (like she had trained John?). John also tried to convince Robert to leave. "Just come out to the car and we'll talk, Robert."

"No, no, please. I don't want to talk. I'm scared. Please, Daddy, don't touch me. I'm so scared. I'm *real* scared. I've been scared a long time. Why did you try to drive me and Mom off the bridge? I'll *never* forget that."

John shrugged off an answer, and indicated he would leave then and take his mother to dinner. Later that evening he stopped by the house, unannounced and unexpected, and went to Robert's room. When he found the door was locked, he knocked. Robert opened the door, thinking it was me or one of "the brothers," and there was his father. John picked Robert up in his pajamas, but Robert squirmed free and got in bed, screaming, "Go away." He pulled the covers up—John reached down and, in one swoop, gathered up Robert and his blanket and took him downstairs and stuffed him in the car. Robert made a break for it and ran across the front lawn; the boys and I watched in horror as John caught him and, carrying him kicking and screaming, loaded him into the car and sped away.

We were all demolished. Poor Robert. What would become of him? Where would John take him? What would he do if Robert mentioned he had visited his grandparents? What a pathetic farewell. Robert called us frequently from a neighbor's, and from the shopping center, and we saw him a few times. It was a heartbreaking situation for all of us.

After John left, the bodyguard observed to me: "That's one mighty sick doctor. One night he took some empty picture frames out to his car, at 2 A.M.! A picture fell out and he reached down, grabbed it, crumpled it up, and dropped it into a wastebasket. I was helping him out the door and I had acted as though I hadn't noticed. But when he left, I got the picture he had thrown away, and saw that it was of Joan.

"And that music! I don't see how you could ever sleep, any of you. One thing that's certainly just not normal is the way he stays awake all the time. It's just like a haunted house."

I agreed; I told him that according to John the house had indeed had a bad history. Several previous owners had met with tragedies. One owner's daughter was kicked by a horse and died. Another owner supposedly choked to death, and there was a spot of blood in the carpet on the steps where, John said, another former resident had fallen, with fatal results.

The bodyguard said he had heard a lot about the doctor, had heard that he had gone to court for permission to open Joan's casket after she had been buried supposedly to get some ring. "My opinion," he told me, "is he just wanted to be sure she was dead! He probably saw some blonde-headed woman from the back, with her hair fixed in a ponytail like Joan's, and his imagination got the best of him. He had to be sure it wasn't her! Probably the reason he destroyed all of Joan's photos was that he couldn't stand to have her looking at him."

He went on to tell me more: "One night he came in and watched TV with me. Boy, he was sure fascinated. It was a movie about a Nazi war criminal who had escaped to South America. He was a plastic surgeon and he changed his face and fingerprints. The doctor was really taking it in. I bet he wished he could do the same thing. He's really weird, m'am, if you don't mind me saying so. I think he really did cause his first wife to die. The smartest thing in the world you can do is to get your divorce and then put lots of miles between you."

The divorce was in the works. Meanwhile, John

made any number of excuses to come by the house, and he called frequently, always with the music of Rachmaninoff or Mozart playing in the background.

While we were in the process of moving to the new house I had bought, we returned to the old house to find John going wildly through the place. I knew we had a problem when I saw John's car in the driveway, but since all the locks had been changed just so this kind of thing couldn't happen, I wasn't too worried. However, in the two hours we had been gone, John had called a locksmith who had already opened the new lock on the front door.

When we went inside, John seemed flustered at being caught and he hurried to tell me he was only there to get some medical supplies from his closet and hadn't had time to get his attorney to arrange for it. He appealed to me to dismiss the boys and the maid, and go into the music room where we could talk privately. I told Mel to get my attorney on the phone immediately, and he in turn summoned John's attorney. His client had literally to be removed from the house. When John saw I was actually moving out, he was in a state bordering hysteria. His attorney reminded him that he was under court order to stay away from me, and he finally got John to leave.

The boys and I were pretty shaken by the incident. John's attorney told him he would not be able to represent him further unless he had his word that these attempts to see me would cease once and for all. As he pointed out: "She could have you put in jail for this, John."

Once again I had to arrange for protection. The bodyguard who had been in the house until John left returned to make certain there were no further incidents.

Several weeks later there was a detailed article in the Sunday newspaper:

THE BIG QUESTION REMAINS:
HOW DID JOAN HILL DIE?

January 25, 1970—The death of Joan Robinson Hill has left behind a bitter legacy, bruised emotions, gossip, unanswered questions, and an investigation studded with strange twists and turns.

It turns out that a brain, brought to an exhumation autopsy in a glass jar, might not be Mrs. Hill's. Medically the condition of the brain does not seem to match that of the spinal cord taken from her body.

But this is only one of the little mysteries in a story that has unfolded like a classic tragedy. A tragedy for Mrs. Hill and for the people closest to her.

The still unfinished drama began when Joan met a handsome young medical school student named John Hill.

Joan was a River Oaks girl, a vivacious and athletic blonde. She had that unmistakable patina of wealth and the best schools, and a warm and engaging personality.

Her great love was horses. She began riding when she was four years old and went on to collect gold cups and blue ribbons by the bushel. About 500 in all. Astride her favorite mount, Beloved Belinda, she dazzled her horse-show judges from coast to coast.

John was a tall and affable man with a vague resemblance to Rock Hudson. He could have played Ben Casey or Dr. Kildare with easy authority. He had already required a polish and smooth sophistication which belied his background as a small town boy from the Rio Grande Valley.

They were married in 1958. For several years, while John completed his internship and residencies they lived upstairs in the River Oaks home of Joan's parents, Mr. and Mrs. Ash Robinson.

When Hill went into practice as a plastic surgeon, the financial position and social contacts of his in-laws were a distinct advantage.

A couple of years ago Hill and his wife and their son moved into their own home, an imposing mansion, just down the street.

The Hills were two of the Beautiful People, making the social rounds. But somewhere along the line, the marriage went a little sour. The Hills separated for a time, but reportedly were reconciled shortly before Joan's death.

On Friday, March 15, 1969, Joan went to the farm and did some riding. Her health appeared to be excellent. That night she attended a dinner party.

Saturday, she slept late. So late that two houseguests, Diane Settegast and Eunice Woolen, became alarmed. About 3:30 P.M. the houseguests asked Hill about Joan's still being asleep, and were assured it was all right, she had taken a tranquilizer to get some rest.

Joan finally got up about 4:30 P.M. and spent Saturday night at home, playing bridge with some friends. She appeared to be all right.

Sunday morning Joan joined her houseguests in the kitchen about 11:30, and told them she had thrown up a Coke John had given her. She ate a little breakfast, but lost that, too. She complained of a chill and diarrhea and went back to bed.

Dr. Hill, as the houseguests recall, gave his wife some medication.

On Monday morning, the houseguests departed, after first looking in on Joan to see if she needed anything. She told them she was dehydrated and asked for a pitcher of ice water.

Robinson, just back from an out-of-town trip,

went to his daughter's home that morning and stuck his head in her bedroom door. She appeared groggy, but told him, "I think I'm feeling better." Robinson left under the impression it was just a case of flu.

The Hills' maid, Effie, returned to work and was startled to find her mistress so weak. She spent an uneasy day at the home alone with Mrs. Hill.

On Tuesday morning Effie took Mrs. Hill some orange juice. "Looked like she was—she was— looked like she was out. She didn't know nothing."

She said the doctor was in the room and told her to clean up his wife's bed, and he left for the hospital. The maid at one point half carried her to the bathroom. Mrs. Hill complained to Effie of "burning up" in the chest, and at one time, the maid recalls, her nose turned blue.

"You pray for me Effie," she said.

About 11 A.M. Tuesday, the thoroughly alarmed maid had her husband summon Dr. Hill home from the hospital. The Robinsons were also called.

They all arrived about the same time, and walked the limp Joan (who complained she couldn't see at this point) down the stairway and out to a car to go to the hospital.

"And I looked at her," Effie said, "and she kind of smiled and throwed me a kiss. And I throwed her one back."

Dr. Hill took his wife to a suburban hospital, when she was admitted at 11:45 A.M. The doctors were told she had eaten some snails the previous week, but had taken no other questionable food."

When she entered the hospital, she was in shock, with a blood pressure of only 60 over 40, and was considered by one physician to be "a dying woman."

Despite intensive medical treatment, she died at 3:55 A.M. *Wednesday, March 19*

By state law, the death of any patient who has been in a hospital less than 24 hours must be reported to the county medical examiner. Sometimes a death is reported by the hospital, sometimes by the attending physician. No one reported Mrs. Hill's death.

Two days later, the county medical examiner first heard of the death when he received a phone call from the district attorney, who said rumors were flying about Joan Hill's death.

The medical examiner called the doctors and hospital administrators and questioned them sternly, then decided the breakdown in reporting had been an honest oversight.

The medical examiner learned that the hospital pathologist had done an autopsy and called him. The pathologist offered to give the county medical examiner his slides and specimens. It turned out his autopsy had been done at Dr. Hill's request. Hill had called the hospital pathologist to come to the funeral home after Joan's body had already been partially embalmed, leaving a less than ideal situation for an autopsy.

The county medical examiner then hastened to the funeral home and checked the body visually, or as much as he could see in the open coffin. He noticed no bruises or other suspicious signs. The funeral was about to begin, and he decided not to hold up the burial.

The hospital pathologist, in his belated autopsy, jumped to an initial conclusion that Mrs. Hill had died of acute pancreatitis. He later learned he had been fooled by a normal post-mortem change in the pancreas.

The county medical examiner obtained the pathologist's specimens of kidney, liver, blood,

*stomach, heart, and brain covering. By these he
concluded that Mrs. Hill unquestionably died
from a massive liver infection, or hepatitis. But he
could not pinpoint the cause of the infection.*

*It could have been caused by bacteria, by a
virus, or by some outside chemical or toxin introduced into the body.*

*His autopsy turned up no evidence of bacteria,
or toxins, so he concluded the hepatitis was probably viral in origin. He found no trace of virus
either. But any virus could have been killed by
the embalming.*

*Hill voluntarily took a truth serum test and an-
swered questions by the district attorney, with undisclosed results.*

*A grand jury considered the case but took no
action.*

*There the case languished for a time, though it
continued to be a prime topic in social and medical circles.*

*Robinson, who adored his daughter, refused to
let the case die. He enlisted attorneys, private in-
vestigators and doctor friends in a relentless quest
to determine why his daughter died.*

*Hill's attorney has charged that Robinson vin-
dictively and unjustly set out to destroy his former son-in-law.*

*In August the district attorney, on the urging of
Robinson, and several others, requested the county
medical examiner to exhume Mrs. Hill's body for
another autopsy.*

*It was to become one of the strangest and most-
drawn-out autopsies on record.*

*The body was dug up from the cemetery and
taken to the county morgue. There, when the
vault was opened, the assembly of doctors saw a
surprising sight—mud smears on the casket.*

It developed that this was actually the second

exhumation. One rainy day shortly after the funeral, a cemetery official explained, Dr. Hill had the body dug up to remove a ring from his wife's finger. The funeral home manager stated that she was buried without jewelry, as the family had been given her ring previously.

The remains studied in the mass autopsy were incomplete. The heart was gone (disposed of by the pathologist). A kidney was missing (used for slides), and a portion of the esophagus was gone (also used for slides).

The brain too was missing. But the pathologist arrived at the autopsy with a portion of a brain in a glass jar of formaldehyde and said it was Joan's.

Each of the medical groups (one group representing Dr. Hill, and another group representing Mr. Robinson) got separate sets of slides and specimens to take with them for study. The body was checked with unprecedented thoroughness. An autopsy usually is completed in an hour or less. This one lasted almost six hours.

Dr. Hill's team revealed acute meningitis, or infection of the brain covering, was the cause of death. This did not square with the medical examiner's earlier finding of death from a liver infection, probably viral.

There was considerable feeling that the brain brought to the autopsy was not likely Mrs. Hill's. It is an almost immutable medical fact, the doctors said, that if a brain covering is inflamed with meningitis, the spinal cord covering will be too. In this case the spinal cord covering, definitely Mrs. Hill's, was clear. The covering of the brain brought to the autopsy was inflamed.

The biggest riddle, one that may never be resolved, still remains: WHAT, PRECISELY, CAUSED THE DEATH OF JOAN ROBINSON HILL?

The entire city was buzzing with the story that appeared in the newspaper. If the district attorney's office had lost interest in the case, this all-encompassing account of the mystery of Joan's death certainly rekindled their fire.

Before we moved, John called me at his house incessantly. When I had the number changed and unlisted, he started driving by and following me. For several weeks the phone kept ringing. No conversation, just music in the background. He would stay on all night if I didn't hang up. Sometimes I could even hear him changing to a record I guess he wanted me to hear.

About this time my father was admitted to the hospital for emergency surgery. He had been bothered for some time with a hernia and we were all certain it would be better to have this surgery behind him. When I was informed, I rushed to the hospital, and found Mother and the doctor trying to calm my father. It seemed his greatest worry was that John might in some way carry out his undisclosed but apparently successful method of eliminating those who crossed him.

When Papa explained to his doctor that Dr. John Hill was about to become his *former* son-in-law, and that he was honestly afraid of the man, the doctor nodded his head. "I understand. There are a lot of people who question that man. Try to take it easy. I'll see to it that you are observed every minute you are at this hospital." The administrator was called and he made the necessary arrangements. The head nurse was summoned and stationed by his side the entire time until he was back in his room and Mother could "stand guard."

As he was being sedated, Papa turned to me and asked if I knew whether or not John actually was in the hospital at that time. I assured him that his light was not on as I came by the doctors' register.

When they came to take Papa to surgery, I glanced

out the window overlooking the doctors' parking area, and John's car was there! Of course I didn't want to further upset my father, so I merely mentioned to the nurse that the feared son-in-law was there. Fortunately there were no encounters, and we were all relieved when Papa left the hospital.

One of the weirdest characters to emerge during this time was a so-called doctor who had no license to practice medicine. One day he called my mother and said it was urgent that I return his call. My telephone was unlisted, and I didn't recognize the name, so I did not call back. At 10:30 P.M., he called my father and said he had important information that could save his daughter's life. He urged my father to meet him at my house and he would speak with both of us.

Papa called me and said he would be there at eleven, and he warned me not to let this Dr. Hagler* inside until he arrived. As it turned out, my father got there before the strange "doctor" arrived. His very demeanor caused us immediate concern. He hurriedly explained that he had information, through hospital sources, that John planned to kill me. He said he was merely a concerned citizen and wanted to see that there was no further violence. He produced tickets for me to fly to Switzerland, where he planned to meet me and watch out for my safety, personally.

Papa and I exchanged glances; we rose and thanked Dr. Hagler but declined his offer, and Papa and Mel ushered him out. Not to be discouraged, he persisted in coming by the house; somehow he got the telephone number, and his calls became more and more bizarre. He claimed to have inside information on John's every thought. Papa had him investigated and found out that he had bought Joan's horse farm, that he was not licensed to practice medicine, and that he was apparently a crony of Ash Robinson's.

* Fictitious name.

I spoke to my attorney, and he suggested I try harder to be unavailable to talk to Dr. Hagler. I had the boys answer the phone during this time; often it was John with his music playing in the background; at other times, this strange "doctor" urgently asking to speak to their mother.

After a few weeks, the boys and I moved to a house we bought in our old neighborhood. When we moved, I tried to keep our whereabouts a secret from John, but he managed to get my new unlisted number and was soon driving by my new house, even though we were in a distant part of the city. Often the boys or I would see him three or four times a day. We wondered if he was there at night, too.

Dr. Hagler must have followed our moving van, because he showed up as soon as we moved in. Obviously he was going to continue to be a pest. Christmas came and the phony doctor had a twenty-five-foot flocked tree, decorated with all the trimmings, delivered to my house. Then he arrived with a stack of gift-wrapped boxes while I was out. I opened the packages and found a gold and turquoise bracelet, some expensive lounging pajamas, and a sickeningly mushy card.

When he called next I asked him to please take the things and understand there was no future in his pursuit of any kind of friendship. He giggled boyishly and said he was always ready to help me, so I might just as well relax and enjoy his company. He claimed to be my self-appointed guardian.

There's no way to describe how infuriated I became. He was repulsive in every way to me. Between his and John's phone calls and surveillance, I was beginning to be more than a little edgy. Once again I had my telephone number changed and unlisted. For a few days there was peace, then the calls from John began again, and in a short time Dr. Hagler was calling. I asked my attorney to take some sort of action. Stupidly, Dr. Hagler had begun to haunt my attorney's office, wanting to have a word about the Dr. Hill case. After a few encounters like that, my attorney told Dr. Hagler he would get a court order against him if he ever called either of us again. Finally he gave up.

I suppose in any case where there is some measure of publicity, the nuts just come crawling out of the woodwork. People seem to like to claim some personal knowledge of those who are in the news.

Dr. Hagler claimed he and Joan had been great buddies, and that he knew John had held him in total disrespect as a surgeon. I found out later that Dr. Hagler never even met Joan or John, but had appeared on the scene to talk to Ash Robinson about his horses, had heard about his daughter's death, and eventually had bought Joan's horse farm. He had been a self-appointed member of the autopsy team, and later had attended every court hearing, including our preliminary divorce and final divorce hearings. I realized I needed to be in a different location, somewhere where people weren't aware of my life with John. I didn't want my business to be of any interest or concern to anyone else.

Robert called from a neighbor's and told me that John had bought himself a white El Dorado like mine, and that he had duplicated everything in our master bedroom. It was just exactly as I had had it before the boys and I moved and I took my furniture. It must have been quite a feat, because the furnishings in our room had been collected over the years, ever since I was a little girl. Robert said his dad had even ordered the exact same bedspread! I wondered why he went to all that trouble. What was the idea? What was going on in his mind? If I had known he wanted my things so much, I would probably have left them. The last thing I wanted was reminders. Most of the ghosts from those traumatic days have faded away, but here I am, still sleeping in the same bed, still haunted by many of the things John and I shared. I would love to have had a complete change of scenery.

After we were settled back in our old neighborhood, Professor Arthur Herzfield, a friend of both the Hills and the Robinsons, went to a lot of trouble to track me down. I had met him one day with John, and I knew he was an old friend from John's medical school days. He was most concerned with Ash's state of mind at that point. "Ann," he told me, "don't let down your guard. Ash is a vindictive person. He keeps saying 'I'm going to *get* John—then I'll get even with Ann!' I tried to interject a little reality into the situation, and told him, 'If it hadn't been Ann who had come between John and Joan, then it would have been somebody else. After all, she was good to Robert, and she was nice to let him come over to visit you.' "

Not to be distracted, Ash had said: "Yes, but it *was* Ann who came between them. Joan was happy till John met her." He went on, "Joan did tell me she had called Ann once, and that she was nice to her. Nicer, in fact, than John was. But it doesn't matter. I hate her for making Joan unhappy. We had done everything in the world for John. They were getting along fine. I'll always hate Ann and blame her for the loss of my daughter."

Professor Herzfield said, "I'm not trying to alarm you, Ann, but I see Ash every week at our poker club, and we are all concerned about this. He keeps repeating over and over: 'Just wait, I'll get even. First I'm going to settle the score with John, then it's going to be Ann's turn.' "

I wasn't surprised, and I appreciated the professor going to the trouble to tell me of Ash's hostility. It was understandable but unsettling. However, I was far more concerned with John's constant preoccupation with my activities.

Months later we came face to face in the courtroom for our divorce hearing.

After the actual divorce proceedings, John came up to me outside the judge's chambers and put his arms behind me, pinning me to the wall. He begged me to please let him come back. He would move anywhere, give up everything, do anything.

Our attorneys were busy talking and a court reporter summoned my attorney, who interrupted the little interlude. I had my name restored to Kurth, and asked for a permanent restraining order to keep John from coming around. Then John got panicky and requested that I sign a statement he hastily authored:

> I, Ann Fairchild Kurth, have no knowledge of the events or circumstances surrounding the death of Joan Robinson Hill.

Fine. I was glad to sign it. John and I were left alone again, and he said, "Thank you, baby, you don't know how much I appreciate your signing that statement."

"No trouble at all, John. I wish by signing a statement I *could* eradicate everything you told me. Think about it: If Joan died a natural death, then only God would know the circumstances. You take the position of knowing something only God should know. This would be impossible unless you claim personal knowledge of the manner of her death yourself." What a stunned expression of realization came across his face.

The grand jury did, at that point, very seriously begin investigating the cause of Joan Hill's death. The mention of John having tried to kill me had caught their attention. They wanted to talk to me as soon as I was no longer his wife.

I still couldn't bring myself to think about the gruesome way he described Joan's death, much less tell a grand jury or anyone about it. If they pieced it all together, it would have to be on some other evidence. I was very evasive in my answers. All I wanted was to be safe, and I had already spent a small fortune on bodyguards.

A couple of months after our divorce John was indicted for Murder One. The charge was "Murder by omission," or failure to provide Joan with the necessary medical care.

The papers were full of it:

> **DR. JOHN R. HILL CHARGED WITH MURDER**
> *Friday, May 22, 1970—Dr. John R. Hill, prominent Houston plastic surgeon, was indicted today on a charge of murdering his socialite wife, Joan Robinson Hill, by deliberate neglect.*
>
> *The unusual indictment charged that the 39-year-old doctor killed his wife by willfully, intentionally and culpably failing to give her proper medical treatment, and by failing to take her to a hospital in time.*
>
> *Mrs. Hill, a nationally known champion horsewoman, died 14 months ago, only 15 hours after being admitted to Sharpstown Hospital.*
>
> *Her tall and dashing doctor husband had been treating her at their River Oaks home, 1561 Kirby Drive, for an illness that grew progressively worse. The indictment by a grand jury climaxed months of investigations and repeated autopsies, including one on her exhumed body last August.*
>
> *The autopsies never established the precise origin of the massive infection which caused her death.*
>
> *Hill's attorney, Richard Haynes, said he had arranged for the doctor to be released on a personal recognizance bond.*
>
> *Recently the doctor had filed a $5-million-dollar slander suit against Mrs. Hill's father, Ash Robinson.*
>
> *Haynes stated the indictment would not affect the slander suit, except "now we'll ask for more*

dough because the damage has increased." He stated his belief that his client would be acquitted and that the doctor would be restored to his place in society.

Ash Robinson declined comment on the indictment. He had pressed for the exhumation autopsy. The pathologists concluded there was "gross neglect, maybe even more" involved in the death. But the medical experts could detect nothing in their tests which may have started Mrs. Hill, a 38-year-old blonde, on her sudden downward spiral into death. She died of a massive, fulminating infection of unknown origin. No trace of poisonous or toxic matter was found in her remains.

I knew John must be a wreck. The telephone calls persisted, always with music in the background.

One weekend my cousin Mary was over at my new house on a Sunday afternoon and we were sitting in the living room. After a while, glancing out the window, she said, "Ann, that is the third time I have seen John drive by since I've been here" (he lived about twenty miles away). I said, "Yes, he does that a lot."

"I don't want to alarm you," Mary said, "but what's the idea? What's he doing? What would he do if you drove out your drive just as he was there? I'm worried. Do your parents or lawyer know about this? Have you told the district attorney?"

"Not in detail, but it's beginning to get to me, too. Sometimes he follows me. Then he calls a lot. Maybe if he didn't see me it might be better. Maybe I should move out of town. Then I wouldn't be so worried all the time about what he might do."

It seemed a shame. Houston was my home. The boys were glad to be back in their old neighborhood. Still, something had to be done.

Soon I devised another "life insurance" policy for

myself. I made an appointment with my attorney and told him how John was "haunting my neighborhood," and calling me a lot. He could understand my concern. I told him I didn't think he had fully understood my fear of John. He asked exactly why I felt I had to fear John.

I told him of the strange "experiment" I had seen at John's apartment. Then about the pastries John wouldn't let me eat. I made him promise never ever to reveal what John had told me just before the wreck about what he had done to Joan. He was aghast! "No wonder you're afraid of him."

I told him I was increasingly concerned, with John's trial coming up soon, and the continuing calls and surveillance. He assured me that our conversation would be kept in total confidence. However, if John should learn that he knew, then John would have to eliminate him, also. On the other hand, he suggested, if John knew that the district attorney knew the whole story, then he wouldn't dare harm me or him.

That made a lot of sense. At least I would have company and wouldn't have to be alone in my fear of John. My attorney reminded me that it would also be a safeguard for Robert. John wouldn't dare turn on him violently if he knew his secret wasn't such a secret anymore.

As our next step, we had to devise a way to let John know that he had more than me to contend with. I authorized my lawyer to tell the district attorney, on condition that if they used this knowledge to prosecute John, they would not ask for the death penalty. I knew I'd never sleep if that happened.

He agreed, and in a few days asked if I would meet the district attorney and tell him the story myself. I first extracted the district's attorney's promise not to ask for the death penalty. He grew more and more incredulous as I described, in John's words, just what had happened.

The district attorney checked with the pathologist, who concluded that the information I had supplied was truly the missing piece to the puzzle. And, like any puzzle, once seen, it was the only explanation that fit. Had I not come forward, there was no way that they could ever have determined the cause of Joan's death, as all the elements used to grow the cultures were natural to the human body.

I found the notes John had made at the medical library, before taking the sodium pentothal test. The district attorney's office researched these notes and found they concerned an antidote to the sodium pentothal.

"We suspected he had found a way to stay awake during our questioning," he said, "and this confirms it."

I described the wreck with John and mentioned that he had thrown one of the syringes over the bridge. This syringe was later recovered by the district attorney's office. After lengthy tests, the district attorney called me and said, "Mrs. Kurth, it looks like you had good cause to be alarmed about the syringes Dr. Hill tried to inject you with. The one we found, if injected into your heart, would have made it appear you died in shock following the wreck. Chances are the authorities would never have checked and found you had received a lethal dose of procaine hydrochloride. Your heart would have quite simply beat itself to death in thirty seconds. How lucky you are to have escaped! Joan Hill was not so lucky. Her death was diabolically calculated and executed. There is no question but that she suffered excruciatingly at the hands of her husband."

The district attorney went on: "I'm afraid Dr. Hill has committed the perfect crime. The only way to ever bring this out in the light is for you to testify, Ann."

That was the very last thing I wanted to do. I was afraid to encounter John in the courtroom. There had been a recent court case in California where the judge and some other people in a courtroom had been shot and killed. I didn't want John to throw any lethal syringes at me!

I was promised as much protection as they could provide, and was guaranteed there would be no prior announcement of my impending testimony.

The district attorney had a lot of questions about my former husband. "What was it about John? Everyone seems to have such a high opinion of him. Frankly, I found him to be one of the most charming men I ever met. I can't even visualize him being unkind or rough, and certainly he's not the kind you'd ever think of as a murderer.

"Even when you talk about him, Ann, except for the description of what he told you regarding Joan's death, and your car wreck—both of which obviously upset you, apparently even you have no hatred for him."

"Yes," I replied, "it's hard for me to realize the John I first knew could ever do those things. He was the most considerate, most wonderful person I've ever known. The fact that he could turn into a person capable of such horrendous acts has caused me to wonder if maybe I'm not a bad judge of character. I certainly misjudged him. And yet, except for those incidents, he *is* the greatest person I have every known. I guess it would have been too good to be true, for him to be *that* wonderful through and through. The strange thing is, those incidents are so completely out of character with the John Hill I loved so deeply, it's actually as though some demon possessed him momentarily. He certainly could revert back to my beloved John just as suddenly as he had changed.

"I think he was completely conscious of the two personalities he possessed," I continued. "He seemed, on occasion, to be trying to intimate there was another side to him. He even jokingly referred to himself as 'Mr. Hyde.' "

"That's fantastic," the district attorney said. "He certainly is a Dr. Jekyll and Mr. Hyde. If he hadn't committed such a ghastly murder, you could almost feel sorry for him. Certainly it makes it hard to prosecute a man who is such a gentleman. Maybe during the trial, something will trigger a response from his other self."

That's exactly what I was concerned about. What if he suddenly became violent?

A few days before John was to go on trial for murdering Joan, I was driving to my cousin Mary's apartment when a woman I had noticed in my rear-view mirror suddenly passed me, turned her car around, and, aiming right at me, crashed into my car and totaled it! Fortunately I was going no more than twenty miles an hour, but even so, my car was completely demolished. The woman seemed quite perturbed when I bounced out and asked if she was all right. The grille on her car was smashed in. Her only comment was, "I'm surprised you're okay!" She never expressed regret or concern, just turned around and drove off. As she did so, I noticed there were no license plates on her car. I wondered, as did my attorney, if that wreck might be attributed to an attempt to "prevent testimony." I guess we'll never know.

When the day came for me to appear in court, my legs were still black and blue from the wreck; to hide the bruises, I wore very dark stockings. One of the newspapers reported "the sultry former Mrs. Hill, the femme fatale in the case, was dressed for the part, in black stockings." When I read that description, I couldn't believe it. Then I noticed that the reporter was a man on whose son John had operated. I knew he was grateful to John, who had been very good to his son; in fact, on several occasions, he had called John to tell him of an impending news story, and he said that he would try to handle any story in a manner that was beneficial to John.

This same reporter friend of John's referred to me as

the doctor's former "mistress." I always thought "mistress" implied "kept woman" and I knew very well that I had kept myself. I had needed nothing; John was always hard put to find a gift, which was why he frequently settled for flowers.

As a matter of record, I was better off financially *before* I married John; I later had to take him to court to collect the thousands of dollars I had given him in case he needed money to make bond. Further, John and I hadn't lived together before we were married. He had an apartment that he kept until we were married, as well as his home on Kirby Drive.

In contrast, the other newspaper reported:

> *Ann Kurth, a petite brunette, was married to Dr. Hill several months after his first wife's death. She is the daughter of Cameron Fairchild, prominent Houston architect, and was formerly married to a wealthy East Texas lumber scion, Melvin Kurth. Her marriage to Dr. Hill ended in divorce after they had been married nine months.*

(Actually I am five feet six—hardly petite.) But that reporter, I noticed, was six feet five, so no wonder he thought I was tiny. I guess it all depends on the point of view. And the reporter. And who he happens to admire.

One of Joan's friends testified that she and Joan had played cards the weekend preceding Joan's death and that Joan had been on a crying jag. Someone had told her John had bought me a new car! Yet another surprise to see in print about myself! I was still driving the same Thunderbird I had—the one I had bought myself when I met John. It was a few months *after* her death that he bought me the El Dorado.

I learned there's absolutely nothing you can do except to sit there and take it. Or, worse still, read it in the newspapers!

John's attorney objected vigorously when the state announced that Ann Kurth would testify next. He argued that "Mrs. Kurth was ineligible to take the witness stand at all, even though now divorced from Dr. Hill, because of the ancient legal maxim prohibiting a wife from testifying against her husband." The district attorney's contention was that Mrs. Kurth could testify to any acts of violence during the marriage, as well as to Hill's comments about his first wife while she was living.

The judge overruled the objections and I was ushered into the courtroom. Several very large Texas Rangers were stationed around the courtroom, and the district attorney placed himself between me and John. And, as he had promised, he kept his eyes on my former husband.

John sat there looking at me. The district attorney later said, "I thought he was going to cry. His chin was quivering. I was afraid you would look at him, and somehow be taken back to the time before he was like this, and decide you couldn't testify."

John didn't remind me of the "happy days" as he stared stonily at me. I was apprehensive as the testimony went on, covering what he had told me, what I had seen in his apartment, the pastries, and the experiment, but I'll swear there was a glimmer of pride in his eyes. While everyone in the courtroom gasped over the testimony describing what had happened to Joan, John listened impassively.

My testimony was devastating to the defendant. John had obviously failed to tell his attorneys anything. They had never even heard about the wreck by Joan's farm. When photos of the wrecked car were passed around, there was an audible sigh from John. His attorney was furious and could hardly wait to cross-examine me. "Mrs. Hill, or Mrs. Kurth, whatever you call yourself now, do you mean to sit there and tell me these are pictures of Dr. Hill's car after the alleged wreck? Why, that car has rust or mud caked on it! Doesn't that look like rust or mud to you?"

I looked at the picture: "No, sir, it looks like blood to me."

He never expected to hear that, and was at a loss for words. But he stumbled on: "How in the world can you sit there, under oath, and say that this could possibly be anything but rust or mud on the front of the car?"

"Because I was in the wreck, sir, and it was a bloody mess. John's nose was broken and my leg was badly cut."

The district attorney resumed his examination: "So the car was wrecked, and you say Dr. Hill pulled first one, then another syringe from his pocket, and tried to inject you with their contents."

"That is correct," I replied. (The district attorney had recovered the syringe containing procaine hydrochloride to present as evidence.)

"Well, Mrs. Kurth, your husband was a doctor. Why didn't it occur to you that perhaps he was administering first aid when he brought forth the syringes?"

"Because he had just told me how he had killed Joan with a needle!"

John's attorney jumped up protesting vehemently. He asked for a recess. Then for a mistrial.

There was no way he could defend his client. The testimony had clearly been more potent and damaging than the charge "murder by omission" would have suggested.

A mistrial was declared and the trial reset.

My cousin Mary and a friend, Angela, who had brought me to court, waited with me in the district attorney's office. I didn't want to talk to reporters so we waited a long time to leave. By the time we got to the front of the building, there was a newsboy hawking a special edition: "Dr. Hill's ex. tells how he killed Joan with a needle."

As we crossed the street to Angela's car, there was John in his white El Dorado, waiting! He followed us around the block, swerving and trying to curb us! We were terrified! What did he want? What would he do? Angela had all she could handle, just driving, with John trying to make us pull over. At one point he was directly alongside us, and I tried to get on the floor of the car. Poor Mary shrieked, "My God, don't duck, he'll shoot me!"

Finally Angela lost him by quickly turning the wrong way down a one-way street, and driving into the parking area of the courthouse basement. I called the district attorney and said I *had* to have some protection. He said they'd keep an eye on John, and that he didn't think John would dare harm me. (He was much braver than I was. After all, he could afford to be; it was me John was after.)

The newspapers were full of the trial.

DR. HILL'S WIFE TESTIFIES HE TRIED TO KILL HER
Friday, February 26, 1971—Dr. John Hill's murder trial ended abruptly in the midst of damaging testimony from his former wife. Mrs. Kurth testified in court that Dr. Hill tried to kill her by crashing her side of his automobile into a bridge abutment and when that failed by attempting to inject her with a syringe. She forced him to drop the syringe, and he pulled another from his pocket, attempting to inject her again. But a car drove up at that time from the rear, and he threw the syringe away, she said.

When the district attorney asked her how she knew Dr. Hill was trying to kill her with the syringe, she replied, "He had just told me how he killed Joan with a needle."

That statement was a devastating surprise to the defense.

After strenuous objection from the defense that the testimony was more damaging than the charge of murder by omission, the judge finally declared a mistrial.

Hill's attorney and his associates were obviously pleased with the court's ruling. As a television crew interviewed the district attorney, Dr. Hill, standing behind the D.A., held two fingers behind the D.A.'s head, in a gesture making it appear the prosecutor had horns.

"Don't do that, John!" his attorney, Richard Haynes, shouted across the room.

The case will be reset within the next 60-90 days.

One of the hardest things I've ever done, but something that I felt was completely necessary, was to call Ash Robinson after the mistrial. I knew he would be reading the papers and would have no way of completely understanding what had happened to Joan. He had spent a fortune trying to determine the cause of her death, and I felt he was entitled to know, and to hear it from me exactly as John had told me.

I called and the maid answered. I asked if anyone was with Mr. Robinson. "Just Mrs. Robinson," she replied, "but his lawyer is on his way over with the newspapers and to tell him what happened at the courthouse."

I told her I wanted to explain what John had told me had happened to Joan. I knew it would upset him, so would she please take him a cup of coffee and check on him to make sure he was all right. When Ash got on the line, I told him there had been a mistrial, as the evidence had clearly been more damaging than the charge of murder by omission.

I asked if he wanted me to describe what John had told me, even though it was upsetting.

"Yes, yes. For God's sake, tell me. I know he did something fiendish and calculated. My lawyer is coming over with the newspapers. He said it was the most atrocious crime he had ever heard of. He said he'll tell me all about it, and that your testimony really shook up John and his attorneys. And they obviously couldn't defend him, because he apparently had not confided in them. What did he do, Ann?"

I told him everything John had told me about the cultures he grew.

"My God."

And the pastries he served.

"I knew it, I knew it. I kept telling everyone. And those girls, their houseguests *knew,* they just *knew* there was something about the pastries."

"Well, that didn't work, so he gave her some ipecac to make her throw up," I continued.

"That lousy bastard. I could kill him! Then what did he say?"

"Joan was begging him to help her, to give her some medication, so he gave her an antibiotic mixed with the concentrated result of the cultures, and as he said, it was just a matter of time."

"Why that *monster!* He must be insane. Only a maniac could cook up something so horrible. I almost had it. I almost had it. I thought at one time he had gotten some kind of bacteria or substance when he went to Mexico. He's got to be put away. Why, little Robert could be next. Ann, my lawyer is here. But I want you to know I appreciate your phoning me to tell me this, and I appreciate your getting up there and telling the world what that goddamned son of a bitch did to my Joan. You must be careful. He'll really be out to get you now. Don't let him. Rhea is a little under the weather, but I will explain all this to her one day when I know she'll understand. And believe me, we're both grateful to you for getting his secret exposed to the world. You're lucky to still be alive."

When we hung up, I broke down and wept. It had been an incredible ordeal, but at least I was still alive. I had to thank my lucky stars for that.

After the mistrial, I heard that Ash had gone to Florida. Robert called and said he had been to see his grandparents; he seemed very concerned about his grandmother, but said that Ash was due back from Florida soon. He told me his grandmother Hill had made him get rid of the puppy we had given him. That little boy had had more than his share of heartbreak.

"Dad is really acting weird now," Robert went on. "He was so mad about the trial. He stayed up all night talking to his lawyers, but they never could get him to say anything. He lies all the time. I can tell when he's lying. I have to fake it that things are all right, but I know they aren't."

The phone calls from John persisted, always with music playing in the background. It was eerie and never failed to give me a cold chill. I was almost too scared to notice whether or not John drove by. I kept the curtains drawn all the time and seldom left the house. I began to think seriously about moving far away. I knew John could find me if he tried, but I had to have some peace. When I saw my fear reflected in the eyes of my children that was just too much!

On one occasion the lug nuts were unscrewed from one of my tires. Luckily, my son Mel drove the car and noticed it right away. Then, a few days later, it happened again. It couldn't be a coincidence. I had taken the car to a garage and they had used an air wrench to tighten all the nuts. Shortly after that, my steering mechanism was tampered with. So I traded in the car, and kept the garage door closed on my new car. That would confuse him for a while! We now made definite plans to move out of the city, and we didn't give out our forwarding address.

I kept to myself, mostly out of fear of causing someone else to be involved, in case John took further steps to see that I never talked to anyone. Of course, it had all been said at the trial. But now the trial was reset, and he didn't want me to testify further.

Most of my friends were more than understanding. Hardly anyone had "the big picture," and certainly no one could comprehend all the things my family and I had endured. There were those who never mentioned a word about it. A few claimed they would have run the minute they found out how crazy he was. (Have you ever noticed how easy it is for other people to claim great bravery?) "There's no way I would have stayed with him!" another friend told me.

Did they think that once John had told me, he would have *let* me flee—only to tell the world? As he had said, "I'll get to wherever you plan to go—ahead of you, and I'll be waiting for you." And now, was he out there still waiting for me?

Another friend asked me, "Ann, how *could* you testify against him? He *loved* you. How could you betray him?"

Doug Van De Mark,* an old friend, asked me to dinner just before the boys and I were to move. As we were seated at the club, Doug asked me, "Who's that man staring at my date like he wishes she were *his* date? Turn around when I tell you. He hasn't taken his eyes off of you since we walked in. Just glance around now—see, the one with his back to the painting."

As I glanced around, our eyes met, and we both smiled; then I turned back to Doug. "That's my former roommate."

"What?"

"The father of my children. Melvin Kurth.

---

* Fictitious name.

Doug was shocked. "You mean that good-looking fellow used to be your *husband,* and you're sitting here with *me,* when you were once married to someone like *him?"*

What a long time ago that marriage had been. At least another lifetime. So much had happened. Was I still me? Could I be, when we got away from all the reminders?

I had made my decision. I couldn't have lived any other way. I had tried every way I knew to keep on loving John, but it was just no use. All the feeling had died when he told me what he did to Joan.

Whatever had been said and done, whatever had been left undone, now it was time to leave. Wherever we went, it would take more than a change of scenery to eradicate the fear that would live with us. "Don't look back," my mother used to say. The time and the miles couldn't add up fast enough. We *had* to be where we weren't being watched by John every minute.

I needed to be far enough removed from the events of the recent past so that people wouldn't be saying: "How could you stay with him?" or "Why didn't you give him the benefit of the doubt? After all, Joan and Ash had no right to tell John how to live his life. If you just hadn't let it bug you, you could be with him right now—and live happily ever after."

Obviously everyone wouldn't agree with my actions. But I wasn't living just for the approval of the world. I felt I was lucky to be alive at all—and I wanted to stay that way. I had to think of myself, for my own good, to say nothing of that of my children.

The last day we were in Houston, the boys and I were driving to my parents' house for Sunday dinner when I noticed in the rear-view mirror that John was following us! When we got to the freeway he zoomed up in the next lane and stayed right beside us, just staring, keeping pace regardless of my speed. The boys were horrified. As we came to the top of a hill, I realized he was forcing me into the guard rail.

A truck was stalled in my lane at the bottom of the hill. I *slammed* on my brakes. The guard rail was on the left, and John was on my right. I had no place to pull over. The brakes screamed, but no louder than the children. I had a sick feeling—can I stop? "Hang on, boys," I cried, all the while thinking, "God, please don't let us wreck!"

The truck inched forward—and I came to a stop where it had been stalled. John stopped just ahead in the next lane. For a second there was no way out. Then I saw a break in the traffic, threw my car into reverse, took a quick right between cars, and squeezed into an exit. John was caught in traffic and couldn't make the same maneuver, and we lost him. We were limp. If we hadn't already planned to move away, we surely would have then!

We had found a townhouse at a beautiful resort on a lake, far from the scene of all the episodes with John. Our place was far out on a peninsula, situated in a remote spot that offered all the serenity I craved. The boys were delighted to get to water-ski and play golf and tennis all the time. We spent hours and days and weeks that stretched into months of peaceful oblivion. We would take our boat to isolated coves for picnics and spend entire afternoons just drifting. We found such tranquility that it was sometimes hard to believe the strange experiences we had lived through.

After a year or so, I heard that John had married again, to someone who taught music. I was glad that Robert would have a mother again. I hope he never betrayed to his new wife any of the *other* John, and that she knew only the good side of him.

Even after he was married, John sent a private detective to our lakeside hideaway. Two men I had seen checking into the townhouse next door came to my door and rang the bell. I looked out the peephole but couldn't see too clearly. They were talking to each other.

"You know she's there. Ring the bell again. What are you gong to say?"

"I'll just ask her something dumb like 'Can I use your phone?' "

There was no way I was going to open that door. I peered out the peephole again. One of them looked very strange, but it was hard to tell exactly why, until they turned to leave. Then I saw he was disfigured and didn't have a nose. He was sorely in need of a plastic surgeon.

Later that evening the sales manager called. "Ann, have you seen those guys in townhouse Thirty-eight?"

"Yes, unfortunately. Why?"

"Well, what's the story on those two? They are asking everyone up here all kinds of questions about you. They cornered me in the bar and asked me every question imaginable. Finally, thinking I might find out at least what they were so inquisitive about, I gave them my card, and they gave me theirs. I said I'd be glad to show them around the property while they were here. The one with the pathetically malformed features is a detective of sorts, according to his card. You won't believe what it has printed on it! The Shadow—Wilson Whiteside,* with an address and telephone in Houston. I don't know how you feel about it, but I'm going to speak to Joel" (the owner of the subdivision).

I thanked him. And then it hit me. Perhaps the man who looked so strange *had* a plastic surgeon. Had John sent him there to watch me?

If so, whatever for?

The girl at the front desk said they were very insistent on which townhouse they would stay in. They

---

* Fictitious name.

didn't want the waterfront, as she first suggested. They would like to be way down at the end of the cove.

"How about townhouse Thirty-five?" she said.

"No, farther down."

"Well, Thirty-six? No, wait, that's taken. Maybe closer to the club," the clerk offered.

They were insistent. "What about Thirty-eight, or Forty?" (We lived in Thirty-nine.)

"No, Forty is occupied," she said.

"When are they leaving?"

"They aren't. That's where the manager lives. Someone lives in Thirty-nine as well. In Thirty-eight the people will probably be coming out for the weekend. They live in Austin. Thirty-seven is taken."

"Well, call Austin and see if we can use Thirty-eight. Those people probably won't be coming out."

So she had to phone about that specific townhouse, when there were one hundred and forty others to choose from. They found they could take Thirty-eight. They moved in all kinds of paraphernalia: camera, telescopes, fishing gear. That afternoon the boys noticed our new neighbors had a mirror set on their balcony at such an angle that they could watch anyone on our balcony. Setting the device up had been quite a feat and required a long extension made from a barstool, with the mirror attached by the wire on the back. What in the world were they up to? The next day, they were joined by a couple of girls. They got chummy with the lady next door to me on the other side, and they pumped her incessantly about their neighbor.

The next day they came to the door again. Mel answered, while I stood behind him. "Hi! We're your neighbors. I'm Wilson and this is Jay. Say, do you think we might borrow some roach and ant spray?"

"I'm sorry, I don't have any."

"Gosh, we have bugs all over. Don't you have bugs?"

"No, we have an exterminator."

"Where is a store around here? Do you all live here? Gee, this is a great place."

"You should just inquire at the office," Mel said. "They might be able to help you," and we closed the door.

They returned later, and I told the boys just to act like we didn't hear the doorbell. This could go on forever.

The next time I left the house, they were waiting on their front steps. (The boys reported that one stayed in front and one in back all the time.) "Hi! Say, we're having a little party, how about joining us!"

"No thanks."

While Jim was at the snack bar, they took his picture. "That's one of them," they said, "that's the middle boy." Jim was incensed, and so were his friends. The marina manager reported they had quizzed him repeatedly about us. "Which is the Kurths' boat?" And to some boys next door: "Is that the Kurth boys' Mach I?" "Whose motorbikes are these?" (sitting on them). Were they going to wire them to explode? Or the boat? Or Mel's car? Or mine? I didn't know what to do.

I talked to the manager. "I don't know what to tell you, Ann, except that they say they are here for a vacation. But they've spent their entire time watching you and the boys, and they spend the rest of their time asking my wife or the girl on the desk or the yardman or the maids every question imaginable about the Kurths. What do you make of it?"

"Nothing I like."

"Joel told me about your former husband, the doctor, in Houston. He said he goes on trial for the murder of his first wife very soon. Do you think these guys are in some way connected with him? We could be facing a real problem. I already asked the night watchman to keep an eye on them. He said they'd already quizzed him about your nightlife: where you go, who you date. Nobody likes this."

"Least of all me!"

"What should we do?"

"Just keep your eyes open, I guess. I've told my attorney. It's just that we're so remote. Is there any way you can get them moved away from me?"

"That's it! We'll say the owners are going to use their townhouse and tell them they have to leave by Saturday." (It was then Wednesday.) Thursday my parents came for a visit. When my father made it clear he was watching them, they finally left.

Another time one of the owners of our subdivision pulled me aside in his office. "Ann, I don't like to be minding your business for you, but I inadvertently found out that Dr. John Hill made a reservation here for the weekend. I had the office notify him that there were no vacancies. I trust this was all right?" I thanked him, and he assured me that the office would maintain a no-vacancy policy if Dr. Hill should call again.

The Houston papers were full of reports of John's trial, which was scheduled to begin again in the fall. His attorneys had had it postponed several times, and I knew John must have been nervous about a second go-round. In their incessant reports about the case, the press kept fresh in the mind of the public the fact that Dr. Hill was still under indictment for the murder of Joan. The charge of Murder One must have made it difficult for him to continue his practice, particularly since he was so self-conscious about the way people looked at him and talked about him.

He had been released on his own recognizance, pending retrial, which made the waiting easier, I suppose. There was much speculation in the papers about who would be testifying against him. John must have felt uncomfortable as the report circulated that the trial was reset for November "when several doctors crucial to the case would be available to testify for the prosecution."

In September, 1972, John had gone to the West Coast with his third wife, Connie. While they were gone, someone called Myra and quizzed her about when her son was expected to return. Her reply that her son would be back Sunday night set John up for a horrible surprise. As he arrived at his front door he was met by a masked gunman, who had already tied and bound Robert and Mrs. Hill, who was baby-sitting. John was shot and killed. The news exploded all over Houston.

We heard the story in stunned disbelief. At last, I thought, this is the end of the nightmare.

The phone rang incessantly. Friends, family, everyone called. "It was on TV, a lone gunman killed John at his front door." The professor who had warned me about Ash's threat called. "Ann, please be careful, he *could* mean to carry out everything he said." Another friend, who knew of this threat, called the manager of our subdivision. "I don't know if you realize it or not, but Ann Kurth is in great danger. Her ex-husband has just been killed, and the person who probably had it done has sworn to get revenge on Ann. Please have the gates locked and the security guard close by. You'd feel awful if someone came to her door and she wasn't protected." All precautions were taken.

All sorts of people were beginning to call, including many that I had had no idea knew where I was. Finally I asked that my phone calls, which came through the switchboard for our condominium, be screened.

At twelve-thirty, the boys and I were just dropping off to sleep, when the operator called. "Ash Robinson is on the line from Houston. Will you take the call?"

With some trepidation I said I would.

"Ann—have you heard the news? Well, they got him. Yes, they killed John!"

"My goodness," I stammered.

"I didn't know what all the commotion was. There were police cars and sirens all racing toward John's. So I got in my car and went down there to check on Robert. Of course they didn't hurt him; they tied him up so he wouldn't get hurt."

"I'm glad Robert is all right. Uh, good heavens, Ash. Right at his front door?"

"Yes, they were coming home from a trip and they shot him. Just right there at his front door. He's *dead!*" He sounded elated! "They taped his eyes so he wouldn't recognize them."

"Well, Ash, thanks for calling. Be careful, and I'm glad you found out Robert is all right."

Why had he called me? But maybe it was a good sign. Maybe he'd done enough. Maybe he just had to have someone to tell it to. After all, everyone was talking about it.

Or was he calling to *scare* me?

Or to make sure I was there?

When the sun came up the next morning, I had a head start on it. The boys had slept on the floor in my room, ready to protect me in case someone came to our door. I called my attorney and we discussed the evening news. I asked him to try to determine if the person killed the preceding night was *really* John. Remembering John's determination to relocate and his fascination with creating new faces by means of plastic surgery, I wondered if maybe he had created another John. I really questioned whether John had actually been the person killed. He could easily have sent someone there and had the murder set up himself.

My attorney told me they would automatically perform an autopsy. But whoever performed the autopsy was not likely to have known John. They would merely establish the fact that that particular body had been shot.

When I went into Austin, I got the Houston newspapers; they were full of the story.

DR. HILL FOUND SLAIN AT HOME

Monday, September 25, 1972—Dr. John R. Hill, Houston plastic surgeon currently under indictment in the death of his first wife, Joan Robinson Hill, was shot to death in his River Oaks mansion Sunday night.

Hill was shot three times—in the chest, left shoulder, and right arm, and his nose was broken. His eyes were taped, apparently after he was shot.

Hill and his third wife Connie were reportedly accosted at the front door of their home as they returned from a medical convention in Las Vegas about 8 P.M.

The intruder had entered the home a half hour earlier and had already bound and gagged Hill's 12-year-old son Robert and the boy's grandmother, Mrs. Myra Hill, age 70, who was staying at the home.

Hill's attorney said he thought it was an outright assassination.

Robert had answered the door about 7:30 to a white man about 25, who said, "This is a robbery."

The man forced his way in and bound and gagged the two with adhesive tape, and put them in the dining room. They said it was apparent the robber was waiting for Hill's return. Before Hill arrived, Mrs. Myra Hill was kicked in the neck by the robber. She was hospitalized later and reported in fair condition.

Hill and his wife rang the doorbell on their arrival, and were met by the killer.

The intruder was said to be unmasked when he first came to the Hill home, but put a pillowcase over his face, with holes cut for his eyes, to meet the Hills at the door on their arrival.

The killer then grabbed Connie Hill, who spun away and ran down the street. In a statement to the police, she said she "could see the flash of the gun" and heard a shot as she fled.

Hill was found by the police, after Robert worked loose and called the operator. He was lying in the entrance hall, shot and bleeding. He died before an ambulance could arrive.

Robert Hill told police he had licked his lips before being gagged "so the tape wouldn't stick as good."

He said while bound he heard his father come home, then heard several shots.

He had worked the poorly stuck tape off by then and, sensing his father was hurt, managed to get the telephone off the hook and dialed for the operator. The boy said the operator helped him in getting an ambulance on the way to the home.

Homicide detectives were combing the fashionable neighborhood late Sunday for any information on the case.

The pastor of Dr. Hill's church said: "It seems a tragic cloud has been hanging over his life for a long time."

Last July the judge who was scheduled to try Dr. Hill for the murder of his first wife granted a request to postpone the trial, because three of the doctors who were to testify were unable to appear at that time.

Joan Robinson Hill died after an illness of three days, and had been at the hospital only 15 hours when death came. The murder trial was scheduled to begin in November.

Reportedly, John Hill had taken out two large double-indemnity life insurance policies just before he left on his trip. Could he have set up his own murder?

After this, I assumed I no longer needed to be afraid of John. I suppose we sort of let down our guard.

The night John was killed, one newspaper noted, he and Connie had stopped at the airport and visited with Wilson Whiteside, "a private investigator who had been engaged to do some work for Dr. Hill on occasion." So the detective who had been watching us *did* have a plastic surgeon. Had John planned to do something else? I guess we'll never know. I began to feel we had been unduly worried over Ash. Surely it was enough for him that John was gone.

Then, ten days later my townhouse burned to the ground! The fire was started by a torch placed beneath the house. Would the nightmare ever end? Once again we picked up the pieces and began rebuilding our lives, badly shaken but glad to have survived another tragedy.

In August, 1974, my attorney called from Houston. "Ann, I hate to bother you with this, but there's a fellow in my outside office who wants very much to talk to you. He says he's writing a story about Dr. Hill. This is the second time he's come to me, asking to be put in touch with you. I told him I would ask if it would be agreeable to you, and I'll stipulate that should you agree to see him for an interview, any passage in his book concerning you will be subject to our mutual approval. You never know how someone else will interpret a conversation or situation. He seems pleasant enough. What should I say?"

I agreed that he could contact me under those conditions, and in a few days the writer called and came to my home, where we spent several hours going over the bizarre events that I had lived through.

"I haven't been able to talk to several people I'd like to interview," he told me, "but I spent three days with Dr. Hagler, and he filled me in quite a bit."

I couldn't believe it. "I thought this was going to be based on fact," I said. "Dr. Hagler never even *met* Joan or John. He is a real weirdo who wanted very much to be involved somehow." I went on to describe the way he had tried to get me to go to Switzerland, and all his personal peculiarities.

The writer was incredulous. He said Dr. Hagler had called him, saying he heard he was doing a story on the Hill case, and that he'd be glad to fill in details based on his close friendship with all the principals.

So far I haven't seen anything about the story this man was writing. He called my attorney when he was in Houston recently and was again reminded that any portions of his story concerning me would be subject to our approval. The writer replied that "no one is allowed to see the manuscript until it is published." I only hope he was able to sort out the facts from the fantasies of Dr. Hagler and the others he talked to.

After a time there were more trials and convictions duly noted in the press.

MURDER CONTRACT ON DR. JOHN HILL, SAYS PROSECUTOR

February 21, 1975—A prosecutor said today the state will prove that a contract was put out to kill Dr. John Hill, the Houston plastic surgeon who was shot to death in his River Oaks home.

The assertion came in the opening statement in the trial of Lilla Paulus, 55, who is charged as an accessory in the slaying of Hill on Sept. 24, 1972.

"The state will prove that Paulus was the go-between in a murder contract on Hill," the prosecutor said.

He said the state will also show that Paulus paid two unspecified sums to Bobby Vandiver, who was indicted as the slayer of Hill. Vandiver was killed by a police officer after Vandiver jumped bail in the Hill case.

Lilla Paulus and her accomplice, Marcia McKittrick, were both convicted for their part in Dr. Hill's death, and are now in prison. I guess someone always wants the last word. Within a few days, another lawsuit was announced.

DR. HILL'S MOTHER, WIDOW AND SON FILE SUIT
ALLEGING ROBINSON HIRED KILLERS

Thursday, March 6, 1975—A $7.6 million suit against oilman Ash Robinson says he hired the killers of his former son-in-law Dr. John Hill.

The suit was filed on behalf of Robinson's grandson, Robert Ashton Hill, 14, Hill's widow, Connie, and his mother, Mrs. Myra Hill. The suit also names as defendants Lilla Paulus and Marcia McKittrick as accomplices in Hill's murder.

Robinson has not been charged in the slaying.

Connie Hill said today she decided to sue "as a means of seeking justice for the death of my husband."

The suit says Robinson plotted the physician's murder out of "revenge and hatred" for Hill over the 1969 death of Joan Robinson Hill, Robinson's daughter.

The civil suit was filed under the state wrongful death statute, which permits survivors of victims to recover damages for negligent or willful killings.

Legal authorities say rules of evidence in a criminal trial in state court require that testimony by an accomplice be corroborated. Prosecutors said McKittrick's testimony in the Paulus trial linking Robinson to Hill's slaying was not corroborated.

A civil case can be won on a preponderance of evidence, legal authorities say.

Robinson, 77, said today he had not read the suit and could not comment on the allegations. He denies any knowledge of the Hill killing.

The suit says Robinson was convinced that Hill had neglected the oilman's daughter, and sought vengeance through a plan to have Hill convicted in court.

In outlining the state's case the prosecutor said that Ash Robinson, father of Hill's wife Joan Robinson Hill, developed an "animosity toward Hill" after his daughter's mysterious death on March 19, 1969.

Dr. Hill was indicted and tried for causing the death by withholding medical attention from her. The case ended in a mistrial. Dr. Hill was killed before the case could be tried again.

The prosecutor said the state will show evidence to link Hill with Paulus and Marcia McKittrick, 24, who is serving a 10-year sentence for her role in the case.

As evidence was presented in the case, the state showed that Paulus's daughter was visiting her mother when a long-distance phone call came from one of Joan Hill's friends, Diane Stettegast (one of the houseguests visiting just before Joan's death). The girl said to Mrs. Paulus: "Ash Robinson is looking for someone to kill John Hill."

Shortly Paulus contacted Marcia and her boyfriend Bobby Vandiver. They would be given $5,000 to kill Dr. Hill.

Marcia continued her testimony:

"Paulus provided us with a schedule of Hill's routine and showed us Hill's home on Kirby Drive, requesting that we become familiar with the area and make appropriate plans. She told us

the number of people normally in the house and who they were.

"We couldn't figure out when he would be alone. He was always surrounded by people."

She and Vandiver made countless trips by the doctor's residence, in an attempt to calculate the best time to fulfill the "contract" on the life of the plastic surgeon.

She said Paulus gave them a newspaper photograph of Hill and his first wife, Robinson's daughter, Joan. Ash Robinson had provided the photograph along with one of Hill which "was cut in the shape of a coffin."

Also she said she and Vandiver went to Las Vegas a week before the shooting, thinking Hill was there for a convention.

"Lilla gave us a $500 advance on the contract, and we drove to Las Vegas."

(Vandiver was shot to death in a shootout with police. He was the admitted triggerman.)

They could not find Hill in Las Vegas and when they returned to Houston Paulus had some new information.

Ash told her that Hill would be in that day, Sunday, and he didn't know the flight number. We called his home and his mother said he would be there about 8 o'clock.

Marcia said she saw Ash Robinson at the Paulus's residence Sunday morning. He informed us that Hill would be back that evening and supposedly had $15,000 with him to pay his lawyer.

Marcia said she and Vandiver were told they could have the money Hill was carrying to make it look like robbery was the motive for killing Hill.

She let Vandiver out at Hill's house about 7 P.M. and went to the Pancake House on Kirby Drive to have coffee until he called.

He called her an hour later and said there had been *"a terrible rumble"* and to meet him at a Stop'n Go convenience store on *"Westway."*

"There is no such street, but I finally found him on West Gray," she testified.

The *"rumble"* Vandiver referred to was the scuffle he had with Dr. Hill before the doctor was shot three times, also the fact that Connie Hill ran screaming from the scene, and the fact that the $15,000 was not found.

Ash Robinson, though implicated in the case, was not indicted. Robinson had apparently pretty well covered his tracks.

Robinson had a physician testify that at 77 he was unable to appear in court, due to a heart condition.

His attorney was put on the stand and asked if *"Robinson hated Hill?"*

Robinson's attorney replied, *"I can say that Mr. Robinson was concerned about what caused his daughter's death and concerned about his grandson, Robert."* He declined to say if Robinson ever told him he hated Hill, saying this would violate his privileged attorney-client relationship.

Paulus was convicted and sentenced to a 35-year prison sentence.

That plan was *"ill-fated and unsuccessful,"* the suit says, and *"Ash Robinson undertook the role of judge, jury and executioner, by initiating a murder-for-hire-contract."*

Robinson paid Paulus about $25,000 to have Hill murdered.

The triggerman, Bobby Vandiver, was killed by a policeman when he skipped bond. Reportedly, the killers had said Ash Robinson told them that there was some woman that he wanted them to kill next.

The suit asks $5 million from Robinson in punitive damages.

It asks $850,000 for Robert Hill for the boy's emotional stress, and the loss of his father's support and advice.

It seeks $1.6 million for Connie Hill for the loss of her husband.

It asks $100,000 for Myra Hill and $50,000 for Dr. Hill's suffering during his slaying.

The suit also contends Robinson has made plans or plans to make transfers of property to deprive the plaintiffs of their damages.

He has advised plaintiffs he has disinherited or will disinherit his grandson.

Based on my past experience, I was sure the passage of time would dim all the unpleasant memories. When I first knew John, I never dreamed that my deep love could ever diminish, but time and circumstances were to make radical alterations.

My love for John died when he showed me the other side of his nature with his diabolical revelations of how he had gotten rid of Joan. Because of the terror I came to know, the John I remember is *two distinct people*, uncannily similar in appearance, but totally opposite in character.

When I am reminded of the first of his personalities, I am filled with a warm and contented feeling. Yet the mere recollection of the expression on his face and the tone of his voice when the traits of his other side were displayed is enough to make me weak with fright. Naturally, I prefer the good memories. How strange those treasured times can still warm my heart (despite all that happened afterward).

How many people had known *both* sides of John Hill?

His brother Julian?

His father?

His friend, Andrew Gordon?

Of course, Joan had.

I think John's mother must have known the two personalities her son possessed.

I often wonder if John could have played a part in Jack Ramsay's sudden death? And I wonder too if the exterminator who died so mysteriously in a nearby apartment had walked in on John's "project" and been discovered?

I gave the district attorney all the information John had relayed to me, and I discussed John's conversation regarding the other "strange and sudden deaths" he claimed to be closely associated with. They had their best detective verify the information, and their findings indicated that John Hill certainly could have been responsible in each case. There was an element of uncertainty as to those listed as "suicides," and in the case of Jack, they simply never found out the exact cause of his death. John himself told me that he had prescribed medication for his father that would be fatal to a person with a heart condition. I doubt that John would have bragged about causing these deaths unless he had, in fact, taken the lives of these people.

A noted judge, who has made a study of schizophrenia and who knew John, held me spellbound as we discussed both of his personalities. It seems he truly possessed a number of characteristics and traits common to a "split personality." He was color-blind; ambidextrous (handy for a surgeon); and he was rumored to have enjoyed physical relations with both sexes.

The judge, who had known Joan since she was a little girl, was at Joan and John's wedding where he met John and his brother Julian for the first time. "An acquaintance of mine was there," he continued, "and he was a blatant homosexual. We had been good friends for years, and he and John and Julian had been involved together in a relationship for some time." The judge continued, "It was too late to caution Joan about her bridegroom, but I was not surprised later at the deterioration of the marriage. They had no way of making it work. Nobody can work with a mind like John's. You can never anticipate, only be constantly observant and cautious.

"The Hill brothers were raised by an extremely forceful mother. Our mutual friend filled me in quite a bit, based on his close relationship with them. I can only tell you that you are very very lucky to be alive."

The judge was particularly fascinated by the fact that John had had to go back to Joan's horse farm, a strong reminder of his bitter hatred, to work himself up to the point of trying to take my life, thereby removing the one witness to any knowledge of his guilt or innocence.

"Did he ever discuss his childhood with you?"

"Well," I said, "he once mentioned that he must have been a very active little boy, because his mother kept a harness on him, and when she took him out, she walked him on a *leash*."

"That would indicate a rather restrictive and peculiar upbringing," the judge interjected. "A person who suffers from schizophrenia cannot have had a happy childhood. Often they have experienced countless rebuffs in early childhood."

"Then," I went on, "he told me that once, when he was quite young, his older sister had caught him in an embarrassing situation with a little girl about fourteen years old. The sister told his mother, and John was whipped until he was senseless. He said he never even thought about girls again, till he was in his twenties and off at school."

John had told me that people used to think he and Julian were sissies because they played musical instruments, that everyone used to make fun of them, saying they were "queer."

"Queer?" I had asked him. "With whom?"

"Each other" had been John's reply. Certainly there had been no denial. Maybe that was part of his personality I didn't know about.

"You know," the judge continued, "John would have fascinated a psychologist. He had a truly gifted mind, and I understand he was a superior surgeon. He did affect an unusual use of language—that further fits the pattern of schizophrenia. He seemed to deliberately try to appear genteel, very polite and cultured, interesting especially when you know he came from such a small community, and from such meager circumstances."

"I know he was considered to be somewhat eccentric by others," I said. "The piano in his office, talking on the phone while performing surgery, playing his stereo in surgery. His music room, his Shangri-La, cost more than the rest of the entire house. He was so obsessed with that place I doubt he would ever have moved under any circumstances. Since Ash spelled it out that Joan was to remain in the house if they separated, John apparently felt he had no choice but to destroy her. That's certainly an overwhelming obsession if I ever heard of one."

"You mustn't feel too disquieted by his attempts against you, Ann," the judge went on. "Thoughts of violence are frequently aimed at individuals who are loved. It's just another peculiar characteristic pertaining to his particular kind of mind. It would take an expert in the field of abnormal psychology to even begin to understand him. He had the true psychopath's detachment from the world, and a belief in his right to do as he wished, regardless of society. And, of course, the morbid traits, such as the manner in which he killed Joan, certainly indicate a sick mind.

"I am interested in the way you described his suspicions," the judge added. "The feeling that people were looking at him, and talking about him. He certainly had good reason to feel that way, I'm sure.

However, those feelings probably caused him to behave in an even more suspicious way."

"I guess I should have noticed some of the peculiar symptoms," I said. "He became so restless and overactive. Sometimes he would go for a couple of days without sleep. Then, when he did sleep, he would sweat profusely. We could never make up the bed without first changing the sheets because they were drenched with perspiration when he woke up."

"I suspect his profuse perspiration was the result of the large doses of amphetamines you said he took. No telling what else he dosed himself with, particularly since use of a needle seems to have been part of his modus operandi," the judge told me.

"It's pathetic," he continued. "His mother's statement that 'Joan's death was an act of God' certainly describes her forceful influence. I know his behavior was carefully cultivated. As easily as he could be charming, he apparently could turn nasty and cruel and even violently hostile. There were certainly a number of bizarre qualities and obsessive compulsions that controlled him. You were lucky to have escaped him."

I often think about that conversation.

March, 1976

I remember how it was, as a child, sitting in the rope swing in our garden. My friends and I would take turns twisting around and around, until the swing was taut—then let go, whirling faster and faster till it was over. We jumped down and ran away, breathless, exhilarated, and free. Glad we did it, but glad when our turn was over, and we could pursue our quieter pastimes.

That summer of 1968 at camp there was a rope swing. The boys were delighted when they convinced me it would be fun to try. "Just hang on tight, and we'll push you out over the river and then jump off when you swing back here." I couldn't believe I had the nerve. And, most of all, I couldn't believe it when it was over, what a relief!

I think I've taken my last wild swing! No more thrills. No more twisting, no more soaring. Let someone else have a turn. That's the way I feel about the past few years. In a lot of ways, I wouldn't have missed it, but what a relief to have it over. To be free. To look back only to the good times. And to go off to more leisurely pursuits. After all that has happened, I know I'll always be overly cautious. I've learned that, and an awful lot more.

I now live in a beautiful lake home surrounded by my sons and five watchdogs, in a house that is virtually a fortress. I am happily residing in peaceful solitude; I really prefer it to opulent splendor.

The story of my life is mirrored in my eyes. The once prevalent sparkle is a rarity now. A closer look reflects the stunned reality I came to know. Even now I feel a vast emptiness. The vacant space—once filled with my love for John—will never be occupied so completely again.

I had an aversion to commitment before John came into my life. After experiencing him—both of the personalities he possessed in one body—you can imagine my feelings and resolve. Never again could I so completely allow myself such carefree happy abandon. There was enough love between us to last more than a lifetime.

And the darker side—the truly sick part of it—has left an ache that will never leave my heart.

Recently I had a visit from my friend Joyce. We discussed all that had happened during the last eight years, with all the various episodes that are etched so clearly in my mind, and agreed we were glad it was all so far in the past.

Joyce mentioned a trip she had recently made to Mexico. When she and her friends had a minor automobile accident outside Guadalajara, the natives sent for the local doctor to treat their injuries. The interesting man who was summoned seemed strangely familiar. He reassured them in Spanish that a small bandage would suffice for their injuries, then he rushed away, apparently very nervous.

At first, Joyce said she couldn't put her finger on what disturbed her about the incident. The man had been pleasant enough. He was rather tall with a heavy beard, and his hair was almost white, although he appeared to be only in his forties. Then she realized that it had been his eyes. At first, there was a flicker of recognition, then he kept his glance averted, focusing his attention on the injuries. He said very little before he hurried off.

"Ann," Joyce told me, "that man has haunted me ever since. I could swear it was John."

I have been unable to forget that conversation. If anyone were able to make the change, John was the one who could have done it. He certainly had the opportunity, and he needed a new identity if anyone ever did. It wouldn't surprise me at all.

According to their statement, his alleged killers were unable to find John in Las Vegas. Could it be John was elsewhere, creating a look-alike? Someone he would send to his home on some pretext, only to have him killed? Maybe John set up the entire thing. Maybe he had himself killed. He was suicidal at one time. After all, he was facing a murder trial in just a few weeks, an ordeal Ash Robinson would hardly have wanted him to miss. What a perfect prescription for the doctor to fill for himself.

I was caught in a reverie about the various possibilities that came to mind when the telephone rang. I listened, but there was no voice, just music playing— Rachmaninoff's Concerto.

Big Bestsellers from SIGNET

☐ **CLARENCE DARROW FOR THE DEFENSE** by Irving Stone.
(#E8489—$2.95)

☐ **.44** by Jimmy Breslin and Dick Schaap. (#E8459—$2.50)*

☐ **NIGHT SHIFT** by Stephen King. (#E9931—$3.50)

☐ **MANHOOD CEREMONY** by Ross Berliner. (#E8509—$2.25)*

☐ **TORCHES OF DESIRE** by Rochelle Larkin. (#E8511—$2.25)*

☐ **GLITTERBALL** by Rochelle Larkin. (#E9525—$2.50)*

☐ **HARVEST OF DESIRE** by Rochelle Larkin. (#E8771—$2.25)

☐ **GLYNDA** by Susannah Leigh. (#E8548—$2.50)*

☐ **WATCH FOR THE MORNING** by Elisabeth MacDonald.
(#E8550—$2.25)*

☐ **SONS OF FORTUNE** by Malcolm Macdonald.
(#E8595—$2.75)*

☐ **INSIDE MOVES** by Todd Walton. (#E9661—$2.50)*

☐ **THE FRENCH BRIDE** by Evelyn Anthony. (#J7683—$1.95)

☐ **THE PERSIAN PRICE** by Evelyn Anthony. (#J7254—$1.95)

☐ **THE RETURN** by Evelyn Anthony. (#E8843—$2.50)

☐ **THE SILVER FALCON** by Evelyn Anthony. (#E8211—$2.25)

* Price slightly higher in Canada

Buy them at your local
bookstore or use coupon
on next page for ordering.

⦰

More Bestsellers from SIGNET